"I can't go through with it," Blake said

"With—with what?" Maggie faltered, but she knew what he was going to say.

"With this charade of a wedding tomorrow. I couldn't—not when Fiona needs me so badly."

He leaned over her, speaking urgently. "It would be dishonest. Don't you see, Maggie?"

She put a hand to her forehead. "I don't see how we can just cancel everything."

"We've got to," Blake said grimly. "There's no other way."

"You mean you'd just walk out on me? It would be very humiliating."

He answered irritably, "No, of course I wouldn't walk out on you." A wave of relief threatened almost to drown her. Then he said, his dark eyes narrowing, "You must walk out on me."

MARJORIE LEWTY
is also the author of these
Harlequin Romances

and this
Harlequin Presents

Many of these books are available at your local bookseller.

For a free catalog listing all titles currently available,
send your name and address to:

HARLEQUIN READER SERVICE
1440 South Priest Drive, Tempe, AZ 85281
Canadian address: Stratford, Ontario N5A 6W2

Makeshift Marriage

Marjorie Lewty

Harlequin Books

TORONTO • NEW YORK • LOS ANGELES • LONDON
AMSTERDAM • PARIS • SYDNEY • HAMBURG
STOCKHOLM • ATHENS • TOKYO • MILAN

Original hardcover edition published in 1982
by Mills & Boon Limited

ISBN 0-373-02546-7

Harlequin Romance first edition May 1983

Printed in U.S.A.

CHAPTER ONE

THE intercom on Maggie Webster's desk buzzed. She flicked down the lever. 'Yes, J.M.?'

The Chairman's gruff voice said, 'Maggie? Ask my son to come along to my office, will you? I want a word with him about the Hong Kong contracts.'

Maggie's stomach tightened. Here we go again, she thought despondently. Another cover-up on Blake's behalf. She should be getting used to it by now, but it still hurt. 'I'm afraid Blake isn't back from lunch yet, J.M. I'm expecting him any time.'

She glanced up at the clock on the wall of the large, well-appointed office. Ten past three. She supposed that when a man was in the process of getting himself engaged to be married to the gorgeous girl of his choice you could hardly expect him to be back promptly from lunch. But it wasn't her job to tell his father where he was, or what he was doing. Blake himself must have the unenviable job of breaking the news that he was going to marry Fiona Deering.

Maggie would definitely not like to be there when he did it, for she was pretty sure that John Morden, Chairman of Morden Constructions International, and a man with a formidable temper, would go through the roof when he heard.

Maggie herself wouldn't exactly go through the roof. Her own feelings were all part of the elaborate cover-up too. She was Blake Morden's efficient and valued personal assistant—the girl he relied on for pretty well

5

everything, except the one thing she wanted him to rely on her for. But that particular hope—always remote—was rapidly passing into history, and would have passed completely when he married Fiona Deering.

The Chairman was barking into the intercom now, and the instrument almost rattled on Maggie's desk. 'Not back from lunch? It's after three, where the hell's he got to?'

Maggie smothered a groan. Oh lord, he *was* in a bad mood; that wasn't going to add any joy to the proceedings. 'I don't know, J.M.,' she said in her low, pretty voice. Everyone admired Maggie's voice and now she made it as soothing as she could. 'I wasn't here when he went out. He left a note on my desk saying he had an important luncheon engagement and might be late back.'

'Oh well, send him along the minute he gets in, will you, Maggie?'

'Yes, I'll tell him, J.M.'

She sat back in her swivel chair. Her desk was loaded with work. All the details of the Hong Kong contract were beginning to come together now, but she gazed at them unseeingly. She would start again in a minute or two; she would do her very best to keep on top of her job until the moment that Blake left for Hong Kong to take on the huge building contract that was his first important solo effort for the Corporation. After that she would bow out as his assistant and he would be on his own—or rather he would have to find himself another assistant, probably when he got to Hong Kong, for he didn't seem to have anyone in mind here in the U.K.

He had been horrified, yesterday, when she told him she wasn't coming with him. Until that moment he had taken it for granted that she would come, just as he had taken *her* for granted in the two years she had worked with him. 'Not come? Maggie, you can't do that to me! How can I possibly tackle this job without you? You're my—my——'

'Right hand?' she had smiled calmly. She had trained herself always to be calm when she was with Blake because if she hadn't it would have been impossible to go on working with him, seeing him every day, suffering the agony of loving him without any of the ecstasy.

He had stared unbelievingly at her, his eyes fixed on her neat, placid face in dismay, and tried to persuade her to change her mind. But of course she wouldn't. Nothing would induce her to work with Blake once he was married to Fiona Deering, only of course she hadn't given that as her reason.

She knew his disappointment was genuine. They worked so well together. They could talk in a kind of conversational shorthand and he relied on her for so much of the detail work, she knew that. Two halves of the same team, that's what they were, he told her.

Well, not exactly halves, she knew. Blake Morden had come down from Cambridge nine years ago at the age of twenty-three with an impressive First in engineering, whereas Maggie herself had a lowly Second from London University. So it was more like three-quarters and one-quarter. But she knew he valued her work because he had told her so, often.

'You amaze me, Maggie,' he had said. 'In spite of women's equality and all that, somehow you don't expect a pretty girl to be a first-rate civil engineer.'

Pretty, he had said! She felt a little thrill pass through her. Did a nice figure and a clear skin, light brown hair that curled naturally, dark brown eyes and a rather too wide mouth—did that add up to prettiness? She'd never thought so herself, but Blake had said she was pretty and it did wonders for her self-image.

That was when she had first started to work for him, and just about the time she found herself falling in love with him. She would lie in bed at night in her small flat near Regent's Park, summoning up a picture of him— the lean, rangy body; the keen grey eyes flecked with green that could flash with amusement or harden into crushing contempt over some business associate whom he considered unscrupulous or disloyal; the dominant, stubborn chin and sculptured mouth with the undoubtedly sensual lower lip; the thick dark brown hair that curled just slightly into his neck; the way he walked, with an arrogant spring in his step—a man who knew where he was going in life and was determined to arrive.

She could see him so plainly behind her closed eyes. And he thinks I'm pretty, she told herself over and over again, savouring the word. Well, that was a start. Perhaps it was the beginning of some more—more *personal* relationship. She would snuggle deeper into the bed, her body growing warm and languorous as she let her imagination wander over intimacies that she hadn't, as yet, shared with any man.

But that was at first, before she had come to take for granted the ceaseless flow of gorgeous girls who had breathed huskily down the phone, 'Will you put me on to Blake, he's expecting a call from me?'

They came to the office and draped themselves languidly over the corner of Maggie's desk, hopefully expecting to be admitted to the inner sanctum—which they seldom were. They waited below in the car park, swathed in furs, or snappy little summer outfits, sitting at the wheel of racy little sports cars. They telephoned incessantly.

And the worst of it was that Blake relied on Maggie to deal with them. 'Tell her I'm busy all day—be a pal, Maggie, get rid of her, for God's sake,' he would plead impatiently. But the satisfaction would be spoiled for Maggie when he added, 'Say I'll meet her at the usual place tonight.'

He never let his gorgeous girl-friends interfere with his business life, and if they showed signs of being too possessive they were apt to fade out of the picture fairly promptly, Maggie had noticed.

Some day, she told herself, he'll get tired of all the marshmallow froth, and then he might turn to a girl who had something different to offer. Something more enduring. Herself, for instance. The closeness and understanding between them seemed to her so important and unique and precious that it was almost unbelievable that eventually, when he had finished playing around, Blake wouldn't want to make it permanent. *Was* it just wishful thinking on her part? she agonised. *Could* liking ever turn into loving? She just didn't know.

Meanwhile the procession of gorgeous girls went on, and each time an affair came to an end Blake would say casually to Maggie, taking her interest for granted as one friend to another, 'We're all washed up, I'm afraid,'—referring to Clare, or Sylvia, or Judy. And Maggie would breathe again and enjoy a brief respite from fear until the next one appeared on the horizon.

Then, a month ago, Fiona Deering came along, and this time it was different. Maggie sensed it at once, from the bemused look in Blake's eyes, from the way he sat twiddling his pencil, staring out of the window at the London traffic below, from the lengthy telephone calls and the even lengthier lunch-hours, and the relief with

which he began to put his papers together earlier and
earlier in the evening. Blake, for whom no business day
had ever been too long!

Maggie felt a chill begin to settle round her heart. She
told herself that this girl was no different from all the
other good-time girls, but she couldn't quite believe it.

Then came the black, bitter day when he said, 'Fiona's
the one, Maggie, the one and only for me. I want you
two to meet and you'll see what I mean,' and Maggie
had put a smile on her stiff lips and said, 'Yes, I'd like
to meet her,' and felt the cold creeping into the very
marrow of her bones.

They had met. Somehow Maggie had managed to
steel herself to accept Blake's invitation to dinner at his
penthouse flat near London Bridge, overlooking the
river. That night he was in euphoric mood. 'My two
best girls!' He had thrown an arm round each of them.
'You two have simply got to like each other, because I
can't get along without both of you in my life. I'm
greedy that way.'

It was an agonising evening for Maggie. She had to
admit, in all honesty, that Fiona was the most beautiful
thing she had ever seen. A body that somehow managed
to be both slender and voluptuous at one and the same
time, curving temptingly out of the scanty black velvet
dress she was wearing. A fall of silky hair the colour of
moonlight, which she had a habit of tossing away from
an exquisite small face, in the manner of the TV com-
mercials. Not surprising, really, for she was, Blake had
said proudly, a top photographic model. Yes, she had
all the tricks, Maggie thought sourly, watching the tip
of a pink tongue passing over dewy lips that parted
slightly in invitation when she gazed up at Blake. She
was so crashingly obvious that Maggie kept half expect-

ing to meet Blake's eyes in a shared secret amusement, as had so often happened in the past when one of his girl-friends behaved in a particularly blatant fashion. But this time he was lapping it up. Couldn't he see the kind of girl she was? Could a man so brilliant at his job be so idiotic about a girl? The answer was clearly: Yes.

The dinner was probably superb, but Maggie wasn't aware of what she was eating. Blake was going out of his way to be pleasant to her so that she wouldn't feel left out, she knew that. But even while he was joking with her, his eyes could hardly bear to leave Fiona's lovely face, and his hands kept straying towards hers across the table.

After the meal they sat in the luxurious sitting room, Maggie in one chair, Fiona and Blake close together on a deep sofa. Fiona dispensed coffee and was sweet as saccharine to Maggie, asking questions about her work, expressing admiration and amazement that a *girl* could be so clever at a job that was—well, not exactly *feminine*, was it? 'Oh dear, that sounds beastly, but I don't mean it like that.' She leaned forward and squeezed Maggie's hands, looking down at the scrupulously-kept, squarish fingernails, devoid of lacquer, and then, complacently, at her own gleaming, mother-of-pearl talons.

'Isn't Maggie simply marvellous?' she appealed to Blake, voicing an admiration that sounded prettily sincere. 'I don't know how she manages it. The right kind of brains, I suppose. Darling,' she sighed, 'don't you find me terribly stupid after working with Maggie all this time?'

Blake had laughed and put his hand on her smooth white shoulder. 'Your talents lie on other directions, my sweet,' he had told her, and the look that spelled out what those other directions were made Maggie wince and say she really must be going, she had some work to catch up on at home.

Blake rang for a taxi, paid the driver, and leaned in briefly at the window. 'Well, what do you think, Maggie? I'm right, aren't I? Fiona's the one.'

Maggie's face was stiff, her throat dry as dust. 'She's very beautiful, Blake, and you're very lucky,' she managed to croak, before the taxi drove away.

There followed several weeks when Blake was almost impossible to work with. He was obsessed with Fiona, but he wasn't sure of her. There was, it seemed, a racing-driver called Pietro Mattioli, and Fiona was having a wonderful time playing the two men off against each other.

Blake took to wandering round to Maggie's flat in the evening, when Fiona wasn't available. Maggie had to listen, with jangled nerves, while he went on and on about Fiona.

He explained earnestly that she was so lovely that people might be inclined to overlook her more solid qualities. 'There's so much more to her when you get to know her, she's not just a pretty face, as the saying goes,' he brooded, while Maggie sat with a fixed smile on her lips and wished she were dead.

At other times he got really angry, and looked a little like his father, the Chairman, as he thumped the table and raged, 'Why does she have to go around with that flashy bastard Mattioli? Can't she see through him, for God's sake?'

Maggie wanted to say, 'And can't you see through her?' but of course she restrained herself. Blake was in love, and she knew from bitter experience that when you are in love you are blind to the faults of the beloved, or at any rate you find some excuse for them. Blake had

his faults, heaven knows, she thought. He had a nasty
temper and he was, at times, too critical, too quick to
judge. But it didn't make any difference to her love for
him.

She kept thinking, though, that it would be wonderful
if Fiona finally settled for the Italian. Two flashy types
ought to suit each other very well—for as long as it
lasted.

Then, at other times, she felt guiltily that she might
be misjudging Fiona. Perhaps, as Blake insisted, Fiona
had hidden depths. Well, maybe she had, Maggie
admitted, trying to be charitable. Certainly, if they
existed, Blake was in a better position to discover them
than she was. She tried quite sincerely to hope he was
right. She even tried to hope they would be happy together, but she never quite managed to make the hope
stick.

If Fiona had been a different type of girl—even if she
had been a beautiful, silly little nitwit who worshipped
him and was prepared to spend her life slaving for him—
it might have been just about bearable. But Maggie had
the strongest belief (which didn't arise purely from jealousy) that under that exquisite, fragile shell Fiona
Deering was made of cold, tough steel all through.

But that was in the past now. Fiona seemed to have
finally made her choice and Blake was deliriously happy,
and he had taken her to lunch today to put the ring on
her finger. Maggie had seen the ring. Blake produced it
yesterday with a flourish, when he came back from the
jewellers. 'How about that, then?' he grinned triumphantly.

Maggie had stared at the beautiful, glittering object
in its tiny velvet-lined case and remembered that diamonds are so hard that they can cut through almost

anything. These diamonds seemed to be cutting through her flesh, straight into her heart.

She looked up again now at the clock on the office wall. Any moment Blake would be back, and Fiona would be with him, surely. Maggie's stomach felt quite hollow. She wanted desperately for the whole painful matter to be finished and over. After a decent time had elapsed she would look out for another job, out of London perhaps, or even out of the country, and begin forgetting Blake Morden. It was going to take a long time.

The office door swung open and she lifted her head like a startled animal. But it was John Morden, the Chairman, who strode across the room and stood frowning down at her. 'Not back yet? Where the blazes has he got to? I've had Forster on the phone three times in the last hour, and a solicitor's time is money, in case my son doesn't happen to know.' The big man looked keenly at Maggie. 'He's not out with that Deering woman again, is he?'

Maggie felt the heat rise to her cheeks. 'I—I don't know for sure, J.M., but I suppose he could be.'

Disgust was written all over John Morden's face. He dropped heavily into the chair beside Maggie's desk and said, 'Yes, I was afraid of that.'

He was silent for a minute or two, glowering down at the carpet. Then he looked up and said suddenly, 'Why won't you go out to Hong Kong with Blake, Maggie? He was relying on you and I was, too. You make a good team, you and Blake, and he's going to have difficulty replacing you. Won't you change your mind?'

She shook her head regretfully. 'I'm afraid not, J.M. My parents don't like the idea of my going out to the Far East for such a long time, and their wishes are important to me.' She had thought up the excuse on the spur of the moment, as soon as Blake had told her that his engagement to Fiona was going to be announced and that he planned to marry almost immediately, so that she could go out to Hong Kong with him as his wife. That had been the end of the road for Maggie. Hong Kong, she knew, wasn't a large place, and it certainly wasn't large enough to hold both herself and Fiona Deering.

The Chairman shook his head irritably. 'Pity! This is a big job that the Corporation is entrusting to Blake, and in a way I feel responsible to my co-directors for the way he handles it. I've got complete confidence in his ability myself, but all the same I'd feel happier if you were out there with him. A man needs a woman he can trust and rely on to back him up.' His eyes grew thoughtful as he added, 'Without my wife I'd never have got where I am today.'

Maggie nodded, her brown eyes soft. She knew from Blake how happy his parents had been together, and how his mother was missed since she had died just over a year ago.

The Chairman's grey eyes, so like his son's, were watching her closely. 'Maggie, you're in Blake's confidence. Has he said anything to you about——' He paused, clearing his throat. 'I've no intention of spying on Blake, or asking you to break a confidence, but this is important. Do you think, yourself, that he'd be crazy enough to marry this Deering woman?'

The Chairman was nobody's fool, and Maggie was a poor liar. She met his worried gaze and said simply, 'I just keep hoping he won't.'

He nodded heavily and his mouth set in a grim line. 'So that's the way it is. I was afraid it might be.' He stood up and she saw that he was controlling his anger with an effort. Something in his face sent fear spiralling through her—fear for Blake, not for herself. 'If he does——' he began. Then his eyes met hers and he decided not to finish the sentence.

He turned away, shrugging. 'Well, he won't be the first fool to ruin his life and career for a woman.' He strode out of the office and the door swung violently behind him.

Maggie sat staring at the papers on her desk. Then she stacked them up and pushed them away in a drawer. It wasn't going to be possible to do any more work today while this devastating feeling of crisis was in the air.

What did J.M. mean by that last remark? And all that about feeling responsible to the other directors for the decision to trust this huge new contract to Blake on his own? In the world of Big Business a man's wife is an important part of his image, she knew that. She also knew that J.M. wouldn't happily accept Fiona Deering as a daughter-in-law. 'A cheap little bit of trash,' he had once called her to Maggie, and Maggie knew then that he must have been making enquiries about Fiona, without Blake's knowledge. That was the way Big Business functioned, and it had always seemed to Maggie a particularly sordid and underhand part of the system. She suspected that J.M., in this particular matter, would be a businessman first, and a father second.

Maggie sighed deeply and for a moment rested her head on her hands. She could see a long dark tunnel ahead into which she was being inexorably pushed, and there was no light at the end of it.

The intercom buzzed again and this time it was Kendal, the commissionaire on the ground floor. 'Miss

Webster——' the usually bluff, organised Kendal seemed to hesitate.

'Yes, Kendal?' Maggie hoped it wasn't someone important insisting on seeing Blake.

'Miss Webster, I think you'd better come down. It's——' the voice faded and he seemed to be looking back over his shoulder. 'It's Mr Blake. I'm afraid he's not too good.'

Maggie stared at the instrument on her desk with widening eyes. Blake was never ill. He must have had an accident, then. Yes, that was it—an accident.

Her heart racing, she rushed to the lift and was sucked silently downwards. As she stepped out into the vast entrance hall Kendal came stumping across to her, as quickly as his heavy bulk would allow.

'What is it, Kendal? What's happened?' Maggie peered anxiously round him towards the desk unit where he reigned supreme all day. 'Has there been an accident?'

Kendal was poker-faced. 'No, miss, I wouldn't have thought so. But Mr Blake is a bit under the weather, so to speak. I thought you'd be the right one to contact, being his assistant, like.'

'Yes, of course.' Maggie was hurrying across the hall as she spoke, trying to take in what Kendal was implying and finding it difficult. She had never known Blake drink too much in business hours; he'd always been wary of lengthy 'business' lunches. 'You need a clear head in the afternoon as well as the morning,' he had said to her often. 'One drink too many at lunch could lose you an important contract.'

She reached Kendal's desk. Blake was slumped in the chair behind it and he looked ghastly. He was leaning back, his head against the wall, a lock of dark hair falling over his eyes, which were closed.

Maggie's hands were clammy and her heart was pounding. She shook his arm gently. 'Blake, what's the matter—are you ill?' She was afraid she knew what the matter was, but she didn't want to believe it straight away. Perhaps it was a virus, the kind that struck suddenly. 'Blake—tell me how you feel?'

He opened his eyes. 'Hullo, Maggie,' he said carefully. Then he put a shaking hand to his forehead. 'Oh God, I feel like death!'

Maggie turned to Kendal, who was standing just behind them, looking owl-like. 'I'll get him home straight away,' she said. 'Could you be an angel, Kendal, and find a taxi?'

Kendal had once been a sergeant in the regular Army and there was no problem about getting Blake into the taxi, a few minutes later. Maggie linked her arm in Blake's, on his other side, and fortunately nobody came through the foyer to witness their exit.

'Will you manage O.K. at the other end, Miss Webster?' Kendal enquired, and the driver glanced knowingly back into his cab and grinned, 'No problem, mate, I'll lend a hand.'

Maggie gave the address of her own flat. She wasn't going to risk Blake being seen like this where everyone knew him, even if it *were* a virus, which she doubted. His flat was one of a lush new complex where the Morden Corporation owned several apartments and housed important visitors from overseas. It wouldn't do for Blake to be seen in this state at four o'clock in the afternoon by anyone he hoped to do business with.

Her own flat was near Regent's Park, small but comfortable. She had moved here a year ago when her salary had taken a big upward swing, and she loved having a place to herself and enough money to make it as she wanted.

Blake lay back in silence during the drive across town, and Maggie didn't try to question him. The driver waited until they had managed to negotiate the five steps up to the front door of the big old house, and then, with a friendly grin and a thumbs-up signal, he climbed back into his cab.

Fortunately Maggie's flat was on the ground floor. She put her key in the lock, while Blake swayed slightly beside her, holding on to the door-frame. Inside, she took him straight into the bedroom and pushed him down on to the bed. He said, 'God, I feel lousy, have you got anything to drink, Maggie?'

She kept a bottle of whisky for visitors and she poured him a small glass, which he tossed off in one gulp. She said calmly, 'You'd better sleep this off, hadn't you?'

He lay back. 'Feel better soon,' he mumbled apologetically. 'Sorry, Maggie.'

He submitted without protest while she pulled off his shoes and threw a light quilt over him. She stood for a moment beside the bed, looking down at him, at the handsome, saturnine face, dark against the white pillow. He had, she thought, the kind of looks that women find irresistible. His eyes were closed and the long, thick lashes rested against his slightly hollow cheeks. His hair straggled across his broad forehead and she put out a hand and smoothed it back.

He opened his eyes with an effort and grinned feebly. 'Maggie love—glad it's you, pal. Don't—go away, will you?'

'I'll be here,' she said calmly. 'Go to sleep.'

He closed his eyes again with a little sigh, and she stood there a moment longer. 'I'm glad it was me, too,' she said silently, and a wry smile touched her mouth as she added, 'I love you, you horror.'

She went back to the sitting-room and picked up the phone to call J.M. While she was waiting for the call to go through she kept pushing down an unreasonable sense of elation. Perhaps she was being too optimistic, but it certainly didn't seem that Blake's luncheon had gone off as he had planned. A man might celebrate his engagement with more than a few drinks, but he would hardly turn up at the office in a state like this—and without his fiancée too. No, surmised Maggie, it was plain that something had gone wrong between him and Fiona, and if that was the case she couldn't be more pleased.

The Chairman came on the line at last. 'Maggie, where are you? What the hell's going on?' He must have heard something from Kendal, but not, she guessed, the whole truth. Kendal was a tactful soul and had a wholesome respect for the Chairman's temper, as had all the employees in the building.

She said, 'I'm afraid Blake's been taken ill. I thought the best thing was to get him to bed as soon as possible, so I've brought him home with me so that I can look after him. O.K.?'

'That's very good of you, Maggie, I appreciate it. What's wrong with him, do you think?'

She drew in a quick breath. 'A virus, probably, they do strike very suddenly sometimes and I've heard there's one of these twenty-four-hour bugs around. Don't worry, J.M., I'll get a doctor in if it seems necessary. And I'll keep you in the picture, of course.'

'Thanks, Maggie, I'm glad he's with you. I can't get round to see him tonight, I've got this dinner at the Savoy. I'd skip it, only they're relying on me to propose a toast. But you can contact me there if you're worried.'

'I'll cope,' she said, and the Chairman grunted,

'You always cope. Don't know how we should manage without you.'

She went back into the bedroom. Blake was fast asleep and looked as if he would sleep for hours. A good thing, she thought practically, that she had a put-u-up sofa in the sitting room. Her mother often stayed overnight when she came up to town for shopping or a concert, and her father, recently retired, didn't fancy driving back home to Amersham late at night. The flat was useful, too, to her brothers, all three of them. Their jobs kept them on the move and she never knew when one of them would turn up on her doorstep. It was always a delightful surprise to see them. The Websters were the happiest of families.

It was a strange evening. Maggie cooked herself a meal and ate it at the corner of the table in the small kitchen, her ears alert for any sound from the direction of the bedroom. When she had washed up she looked in again and Blake was still sleeping, so she made coffee and sat down in front of the T.V. She watched every programme doggedly through, jumping each time a gun fired, but hadn't the faintest idea who was shooting whom.

Soon after the close-down she thought she heard a stirring in the bedroom and went to the kitchen to put the coffee percolator on. She was carrying it into the sitting room, with cups on a tray, when Blake appeared in the doorway. His dark hair was tousled and his face was dreadfully pale, with dark rings under his eyes. Maggie felt shocked; she always thought of Blake as being extremely fit. It was painful to see him looking like this, and with desperation written all over his face, too. But he was quite evidently sober again.

He looked at Maggie, sitting on the sofa in a blue cotton wraparound, which she had procured from the bedroom on one of her visits there to check whether he was still sleeping.

'So,' he said rather nastily, 'little Maggie was the good Samaritan who stepped in and offered sanctuary. I trust I didn't put you to too much inconvenience.'

'Don't be silly, Blake,' Maggie said shortly. 'Sit down and have some black coffee. You look as if you need it.'

'I'll have a small drink with it,' he said, '*with* your permission, of course.' He went over to the cupboard where she kept the drinks. 'O.K., O.K., there's no need to look at me like that! I'm not going to get tight again, so don't worry.' She might have been a nagging wife, the way he glared at her. 'Another small drink is the best way to complete the cure. Or weren't you familiar with all these sordid little ploys? Good little Maggie,' he sneered. 'Never overstep the mark, do you?'

She winced as if he had struck her. She had always thought he liked her, that they were real friends, and all the time he was thinking of her as a colourless little goody-goody. Perhaps he had laughed at her with his girl-friends. It hurt badly.

'All right, don't go on about it.' She poured a cup of black coffee and held it out to him. 'You're obviously in a foul temper about something, so the best thing you can do is to drink this and then go. I only brought you here because I didn't want your father, or anyone connected with the company, to see you in the state you were in, in the middle of the afternoon. But now you've sorted yourself out, the sooner you leave the better.'

He took the coffee from her, his eyes fixed on her small, composed face, and couldn't have guessed at the raging misery that was trying to break down her usual calmness.

'You've never spoken like that to me before,' he said, frowning.

'You've never been abominably rude to me before.' She stood up, the picture of a hostess giving a plain hint to a guest who has overstayed his welcome.

But Blake didn't stand. He put down his cup and groaned, running a hand through his rough, dark hair.

'O.K., Maggie, so I'm behaving bloody badly. I know that darned well. I suppose I just expected you to understand, you always *do* understand.'

She gaped at him. 'Understand what?'

He said, with an unpleasant glint in his eye, 'No, of course you wouldn't. You don't know, do you?' He put a hand in his pocket and pulled out a crumpled sheet of violet-coloured paper. 'This was waiting for me when I got to the Grill Room. Go on, read it.'

Maggie smoothed out the paper and read, written in a flamboyant hand in purple ink: 'Married Pietro this morning. When you get this we'll be in Rome. Sorry it didn't work out, darling, but lots of love all the same. Fiona.'

She folded the paper neatly and handed it back to him, shocked by the violence of her relief. 'I—I don't know what to say, Blake.' She couldn't very well say, Congratulations, you've had a lucky escape. Instead she said, 'You must feel badly about it, and I'm very sorry.' That sounded stupidly prim, but it was the best she could manage.

'Badly!' He laughed bitterly. 'I damned near walked across the Embankment and tipped myself into the river! Instead, as was crashingly obvious, I stayed where I was and went on drinking until the pain went away.' He glared at her, 'And don't you dare nag at me, Maggie Webster. You don't know what it feels like to love someone like that.'

Don't I indeed? she thought. Her eyes rested on his lean cheeks and the line of his mouth, firm and yet oddly sweet, and she felt weak with longing. She said, 'Possibly not. But I wasn't going to nag.'

'No? That's how it looked to me. A regular nanny act you put on, didn't you? Lugging me here and keeping watch over me until the effect of all that nasty drink wore off!'

His tone was cruelly sarcastic and she wondered how much more she could take. Even making allowances for the state of his emotions, and the natural desire to hit back at anyone within range, there was a limit to the amount of punishment she could endure.

She put down her coffee cup and leaned towards him. 'Look, Blake,' she said, keeping her voice calm with a great effort, 'I really had no intention of nannying you. In fact, I wasn't really considering *you* at all. All I wanted was to remove you from the building before you did any harm to the company's reputation—which I care about myself, being an employee.'

He laughed shortly. 'Very worthy of you! Please accept my grateful thanks on behalf of Morden Constructions. In future I shall take care to give the right impression to all the customers.'

He got to his feet, quite steadily now. Blake Morden was himself once more—tall and dark and arrogant and responsible to nobody for his actions. 'I won't embarrass you with my presence any longer, Maggie.'

She glanced at her watch, which said twenty minutes past midnight. She couldn't help asking, 'Where will you go?'

'Don't worry,' he mocked. 'The Thames is unpleasantly cold at this time of night. I shall return to my own four walls and drown my sorrows in private.'

She hadn't time to consider. She jumped to her feet and put a restraining hand on his arm. 'Blake,' she pleaded, 'don't go!'

He was suddenly very still, looking down at her with a strange expression in his grey-green eyes. 'What is this, Maggie? You're not offering consolation, are you? Would you stretch your loyal service to taking me into your bed to provide relief and solace?' The mockery was in his voice still, but now it was no longer unkind.

'I—I——' she stammered, 'I didn't really think of it like that—I only wanted to—to——'

To what? she thought, her heart beating wildly. What had she done? Had she let him see that she was crazily in love with him? She felt the hot blood surging into her cheeks.

He shook his head, rather as if he were refusing an unattractively sticky sweet from a small child. 'Thanks for the offer, Maggie, but it wouldn't do.'

'No, I suppose not,' she said in a practical voice, as wave after wave of humiliation threatened to drown her. At least he had been kind enough to say '*it* wouldn't do,' and not '*you* wouldn't do.' But of course she wouldn't do, not after Fiona.

She grinned up at him with a fine carelessness, thinking how merciful it was that she had practised for so long the way to mask her feelings. 'It was just a thought—forget it.'

'It was a friendly thought,' he said.

There was a somewhat awkward little silence and then he said suddenly, 'There *is* something you could do for me, though.'

'Yes?' she said brightly.

'You could come out to Hong Kong with me on this assignment.'

'Oh!' That took her completely by surprise. 'Well, I— my parents, you see——' She was wondering quite desperately how she could reasonably change her mind. There was nothing, now, to stop her going with him, working with him, seeing him every day. And yet she had refused so definitely and made out such a good case for refusing. What an impulsive idiot she had been! She could have wept.

He was watching her face intently. Then he said, 'I could think of one way of getting you out there. If we were married, your parents couldn't very well object, could they?'

'Married?' Her head jerked back and her mouth fell a little open. 'Did you say *married*? But we couldn't—you couldn't! You don't love me.'

His mouth twisted grimly. 'I can hardly deny that, after this afternoon's little episode. But does love matter all that much? You don't love me either. We get along splendidly together and we work as one person, as you very well know. It seems such a pity to waste all that. Maybe——' he smiled and to Maggie his smile looked positively ghoulish—'maybe we would wake up one morning and find we'd fallen in love!'

She could think of nothing to say or do except to throw her arms round him and tell him she loved him already, that she'd been crazy about him for ages and ages. She could just imagine his horror if she did. No, this was something she had to handle carefully, she thought, trying to pull her scattered wits together. One false slip and the whole dazzling picture that was taking shape before her eyes would dissolve into nothingness.

Blake said, 'There isn't anyone else, is there? You'd have told me.'

She shook her head dumbly. Nobody that mattered. There was Nicholas Grant, the Corporation's head architect, who had asked her out to dinner once or twice. He was an older man, pleasant, easy to talk to, divorced about a year ago. Sometimes Maggie had wondered whether their occasional dates were leading up to anything more, but she wouldn't have considered marrying Nicholas when she was in love with Blake.

'Well then——' urged Blake and now there was a strange, hard, almost reckless note in his voice. 'How about it Maggie? Shall we try and make a go of it together?'

She still hesitated, frowning, pretending to consider. Then she looked up and met his grey-green eyes, and they were gleaming just as they did when he had come up with a brilliant solution to some difficult problem in his work. She grinned as if they were sharing a good joke. 'I'll risk it if you will,' she said, and didn't know whether she was being given a passport to heaven or signing her own death warrant.

CHAPTER TWO

BLAKE held out his hand. 'Shake, partner,' he invited with a twisted grin. Maggie put her hand in his and felt a tingle run right up her arm. She suddenly realised that although they had been working together all this time Blake had never before touched her deliberately, and now the feel of his skin, cool and hard against hers, was terribly disturbing.

He released her hand casually. 'That's settled, then. Tomorrow we'll break the glad news. Meanwhile, you'd better have this.' He felt in his pocket and brought out the huge diamond cluster ring he had shown her yesterday. 'Let's see if it fits,' he said carelessly, reaching for her left hand.

She recoiled as if he were offering her a cup of poison. 'N-no,' she stammered. 'Not that one. It—it wouldn't suit me at all.'

He raised his dark eyebrows impatiently. 'How do you know when you haven't tried it on?'

She stared down at the diamonds, glittering in the overhead light. This was the ring he had bought for Fiona with such loving anticipation. How could he pass it on to her so casually? She had never suspected Blake of being sentimental, but this was too much altogether.

'It's not my sort of ring at all,' she insisted, feeling almost physically sick at the thought of wearing the ring he had chosen for another girl. 'I'd rather have something—something plainer.'

He lifted her hand and looked down at the slim, brown, useful-looking fingers. He shrugged. 'You're probably right. You'd better go along tomorrow and choose one you like. I'll give you a note for Garrard's.'

He might have been telling her to order a load of hardcore, she thought dispiritedly, but immediately took herself to task. She mustn't expect more from Blake than he had offered. In fact, she mustn't expect anything at all from him, other than their usual friendly business partnership. She must take things as they came. Perhaps he would forget Fiona in time—men did forget women more easily than the other way round, she had heard. Then her chance might come.

'O.K.,' she said calmly, 'I'll do that. I promise not to break your bank account,' she added flippantly, and then wished she hadn't.

His face darkened. 'Oh, for Pete's sake don't come the frugal little wife already!' he burst out irritably. 'I can't take that sort of thing.'

'All right, I won't,' she said cheerfully. 'I'm sure I can be as extravagant as the next girl. Just don't faint when you get the bill, that's all.'

Blake was looking round the sitting room and she could see that he had already lost interest in the subject. 'Mind if I kip down here for the remainder of the night?' He nodded towards the sofa, which Maggie had already extended to make into a bed. 'Seems hardly worth while turning out again.' His mouth twisted. 'It's permissible, surely, now that we're respectably engaged.'

'I expect so,' she said shortly. She hoped he would soon stop infusing irony into everything he said to her. 'I'll get you some blankets.'

She turned to the door into the bedroom, but suddenly he was there before her. He put both hands on her arms and looked down into her face. 'Put up with me for a while, Maggie dear,' he said. 'I'm asking a lot of you, but one day I'll make it up to you somehow. Just give me time.'

She smiled at him, and if he had been in the mood to look hard at her he might have been surprised by the blazing message of love in her face. She turned away quickly. 'All right,' she said lightly. 'I'll hold you to that.'

Blake was stretched out on the sofa when she came back with the blankets. It was warm in the flat on this June night, and she threw one blanket loosely over him. He opened his eyes as if it hurt to do so. ''night,

Maggie,' he murmured, and closed them again. She saw that he was almost asleep again already.

'Goodnight, Blake.' She touched his dark, unruly hair and then bent impulsively and rubbed her cheek against it, smelling the astringent scent of the cologne he always used. It gave her an odd, tingling sense of intimacy.

He didn't stir, and she went into her bedroom and closed the door. She sat at the dressing table, staring at herself in the mirror and trying to come to terms with the situation. Would Blake have changed his mind in the morning in the cold light of day, when he was completely sober? And if he hadn't—if, for the sake of his career and the work they were doing together, he still wanted to marry her, would he ever love her? Would she ever see him look at her as he had looked at Fiona, as if she were the most precious thing in the whole world?

Certainly she couldn't hope to compete with Fiona where looks were concerned. She stared critically at her reflection. Curly light brown hair, soft brown eyes (one young man who had cherished a romantic yearning for her in her teens had called them 'eyes like wallflowers in the rain', which had made her giggle); a fine skin that tanned smoothly but at the moment was pale because she had been working too hard to get out in the sunshine; a mouth that curved so easily into a smile that people were inclined to overlook the firmness of the small, square chin below it.

No, she decided sanely, no man would ever be dazzled by her looks. But Blake had once said she was pretty, and no doubt her appearance could be improved. When she was Blake's wife (*if* she was Blake's wife, she amended, for as yet she couldn't quite believe it) she would presumably have more time to spend on her appearance, and more incentive to look nice for him.

Blake's wife! Second-best, of course, but she didn't care, she would take him on any terms whatever. She slid out of her clothes, creamed her face carefully and cleaned her teeth even more thoroughly than usual. As she slipped under the bedcover she thought she was too excited to go to sleep, but oddly enough she began to feel drowsy almost immediately. Her last waking thought was, 'Please don't let him change his mind. Please let it come true!'

In the days that followed it looked as if her prayer had been answered, because Blake showed no sign of changing his mind. Neither did he show any signs of being heartbroken. Only Maggie knew that behind the unflagging energy and almost frenetic drive with which he threw himself into his work was a desperate need to drain himself of feeling. He was like a man who has closed the door on a forbidden dream and was exerting all his energy to keep it closed.

Everyone was delighted when the engagement was announced. Maggie's father, who was in the construction industry himself and had had amicable business dealings with John Morden, showed his pleasure in a practical manner by presenting Maggie with a substantial cheque 'to go on a shopping spree.' Maggie's mother, a tiny, soft-spoken woman who didn't look capable of coping with the upbringing of three hefty sons and a tomboy daughter, but had managed it extremely successfully, was over the moon. 'A wedding at last!' she rejoiced gleefully. 'A real wedding that I can organise myself. Boys are a total loss in that respect.' All three of her sons were married—two of the weddings had been at register offices, much to Mrs Webster's disgust, and the other son had been married out in New Zealand, where he was working at the time. 'What a blessing it is to have a daughter! We must go and see the vicar tomorrow if the wedding is to be inside a month. You can't start too soon if you want things to run smoothly. Now I shall go and write some letters and spread the good news.'

She kissed Maggie with tears in her eyes. 'My darling girl, I can't tell you how happy I am for you. Blake Morden's a splendid young man, your father has always said. You must bring him to supper tomorrow, so that I can get to know him better.'

Blake had pulled a very rueful face at the prospect of a church wedding, but he agreed with fairly good grace when Maggie said, 'I can't deny Mother the thrill, and she hates the idea of a register office.'

'And what about you?' Blake had questioned her in the ironic voice he kept for the subject. 'Do you long for the blessing of the higher powers upon our union?'

'Yes, I do,' Maggie said quietly. 'I think it will make it seem more real.'

He eyed her curiously. 'It doesn't seem real to you yet?'

'No, I'm afraid it doesn't.' She shook her head.

For once he was giving her his full attention. He said slowly, 'I'm being a selfish bastard in offering you such a bad bargain, Maggie. You deserve something better than a makeshift marriage.' His brow was creased suddenly into a row of furrows. 'Are you sure you still want to go through with it?'

Panic shook her. Was he leading up to calling it off? But she managed to keep her voice placid as she replied. 'Oh yes, I don't like changing my mind once I've decided on something. I hate an anticlimax.'

He smiled and she felt comforted that he didn't pursue the subject. Evidently he had no regrets, and nobody but she herself was aware of his lack of enthusiasm for their impending wedding. To everyone else he was a happy man, and if he seemed less than eager to accept invitations to the usual celebration parties, it could be explained by the fact that the couple were flying out to the Far East for their honeymoon, after which Blake was starting on an important new project there, and that he was wildly busy getting through the preliminary work.

That went for Maggie too. Blake heaped the work on her and she thought rather wryly that he was certainly getting his money's worth. Meetings—long reports—telephone calls out to Hong Kong at all hours of the night—and sometimes even in the middle of the night. On the nights she slept at home she plugged the phone in beside her bed, and when her mother demurred that she would be tired out, she grinned and said that Hong Kong wouldn't change its time-zone to suit her.

In between, she managed shopping trips with her mother, and tried to believe that this was a real marriage and that Blake would be interested in what she was buying. Sometimes she almost managed to believe it. It was fun buying all the pretty, light dresses she would be needing, and only when her mother started talking about honeymoon nighties did she feel hollow inside, realising that she hadn't the faintest idea whether Blake would want to make it a real honeymoon or not. He hadn't even mentioned that side of it, and she wasn't brave enough to ask him. So she submitted to her mother's happy suggestions of chiffons and wisps of silk in delicate pastel colours, and tried not to think too much about the occasions when she would wear them.

The weeks slipped past and the wedding preparations, under Mrs Webster's capable direction, went on without a hitch. Invitations were sent out, presents started to arrive at the big family house in Amersham, caterers were booked. Maggie, still living at her flat in London, to be near the office, went home as often as she could manage, but by and large she was happy to leave everything to her mother, who was enjoying it all so enormously.

A fortnight before the date of the wedding Maggie had her first fitting for her wedding dress. 'Do you think it's quite *me*?' she asked her mother with a doubtful grin, touching the delicate ivory silk lace with one brown, square-tipped finger.

'Of course it is, my darling,' Mrs Webster assured her, with an encouraging little hug. 'You'll look beautiful, and Blake will be more in love with you than ever.' Maggie thought very wryly that that shouldn't be difficult, as he wasn't in love with her at all. But nobody must know that, except Blake and herself.

It was arranged that there should be two bridesmaids, the young daughters of Maggie's eldest brother, James, who was bringing his family down from Scotland for the wedding. Mrs Webster had long telephone conversations with her Scottish daughter-in-law, Catriona, about the girls' dresses, and it was finally decided that they should wear shell-pink organdie. 'They'll look simply adorable in pink, with their dark hair,' Mrs Webster enthused to Maggie. 'And I think it would be a lovely touch to have one or two very pale pink rosebuds among the cream ones in your bouquet.'

Maggie's middle brother, David, was stationed in London at present, so his attendance with his wife Lucy presented no problem. But the greatest thrill of all was when a phone call came from New Zealand announcing that Ian, the youngest brother, had decided to bring forward his leave and fly home with his wife for the occasion. That, of course, made Mrs Webster's happiness complete.

'All my family together again!' She sobbed tears of joy into her handkerchief, and Maggie hugged her and shared her pleasure. It would be wonderful to see Ian and Joyce again.

Sometimes Maggie sat in her bedroom at night and stared at the square-cut emerald on her engagement finger (the ring she had chosen by herself, and which she considered suited her slim, capable hand) and wondered if it were all part of some complicated dream. Her relationship with Blake was much the same as it had always been, that of friends and colleagues, and it was almost impossible to believe that in a few days' time she would be his wife. Neither of them spoke of the events of the day that Fiona had got married. It would have been nice to infer that he was getting over it, Maggie thought, but she knew he wasn't. Blake had changed; he was throwing himself headlong into his work, but when he wasn't working there were lines of strain around his mouth, and his temper was more than usually erratic, although he never lost his temper with Maggie herself.

Maggie went on working at the office, and it looked as if she would be working up to the very last moment. She and Blake were leaving for Hong Kong immediately after the reception and all the loose ends of the contract had to be tied up before then. To make matters more complicated, Blake had to fly to New York unexpectedly, to iron out some snags that had arisen with one of their sub-contractors there, and his absence left even more for Maggie to cope with. She had J.M. to consult, of course, if she was in doubt, but he was deeply involved with plans for a new factory to be built in East Anglia, and wasn't always available.

Three days before the wedding, however, he returned from a trip to Ipswich and, finding Maggie still at the office at seven o'clock, insisted on her calling it a day and going out to dinner with him.

He took her to his favourite restaurant in the City, and they ate mixed grills and J.M. ordered a bottle of Chablis, and they talked of the Hong Kong contract.

'It's one of the biggest things we've undertaken, Maggie, as you well know. Fascinating, because the buildings will be partly on reclaimed land. It's amazing, when you come to think of it, how it's possible to flatten a good-sized hill and just dump it into the sea and then build on it. But you know all about that yourself, of course.'

'Only in theory. I can't wait to see how it works in practice.' Maggie's brown eyes were sparkling, her cheeks a little flushed with the good food and wine, and J.M. thought complacently what a wise fellow his son was to pick a pretty, intelligent girl like Maggie Webster.

They had finished dinner and were lingering over coffee and liqueurs. J.M. lit a large cigar and beamed on Maggie. 'A real working wife, you're going to be, my girl, and a treasure to my son.' He smiled his broad, twinkling smile. 'Blake knew what he was doing when he chose you for a wife. You mustn't let him work you too hard, though. He's a demon when he really gets his teeth into a job.'

Maggie nodded. 'Don't I know it? And he's really keen on this one.'

The Chairman puffed thoughtfully at his cigar for a while and then leaned forward confidentially. 'You know, my dear, I was scared stiff Blake was going to make a fool of himself over that Deering woman, but I should have had more confidence in his good sense. He's sowed a few wild oats, I grant you that, but he knew when the time had come to settle down. He takes after his dad.' He chuckled. 'I had an eye for a pretty girl myself when I was a young man, but once I married my dear wife there was never any other woman in my life. We had thirty years together,' he mused. 'Thirty good years.'

He lapsed into silence and Maggie knew he was remembering times that had gone for ever. Presently he looked up and said suddenly, 'You know, Maggie, if Blake *had* been stupid enough to marry the Deering woman it would have been the end of his involvement with the Hong Kong contract. The Directors would never have agreed to his taking her out there as his wife. She was—and this is in confidence, mind,—she was mixed up in a nasty little scandal out there last year. I needn't go into details, but it seems she was involved with a fellow who had links with one of the notorious Triad gangs. You've heard of the Triads, of course—the Hong Kong Mafia. I don't say that the girl was actively working for them, but she was sufficiently in with them to make her absolutely unacceptable to our friends out there.'

Maggie digested this information. 'I didn't know,' she said finally, rather lamely. 'I don't think Blake knew about it, did he?'

J.M. shook his massive grey head. 'I shouldn't imagine so, but if he *had* been serious about her he would have had to know. He'd have had to choose between that woman and his career with the Corporation, that's what it boils down to.' His face was stern now, the bushy brows drawn together. 'It would have been a blow to me, I can tell you. I don't say he would have been sacked, he's far too valuable for that, but it would have been a severe setback to his upward climb in the profession. You know, Maggie, I'd dearly like to see him take my place, some day, and I know he could do it.' His expression relaxed, his eyes shone with pride in his son. 'With you as a wife, my dear, there'll be no stopping him.'

He insisted on driving her back to Amersham, where he came in for a chat with her parents before leaving. It was all so friendly, pleasant and *normal*, Maggie thought, as she watched the big car disappear round the corner of the drive, with its owner waving cheerily out of the window. Everyone was so pleased. If only they knew that it was just a sham—a makeshift marriage, Blake had called it—how hurt and distressed they would be! She was living a lie, and she hated it, it was quite foreign to her nature, but once the wedding was over and they had left for Hong Kong that part of it would be finished. Then it would be up to her to try to turn the makeshift marriage into a real, worthwhile relationship. She hadn't a clue as to how she was going to do it, and there had been no time to think it out, but somehow—*somehow*—she determined, she would win through, once she was Blake's wife.

All at once, it seemed, the Saturday of the wedding was nearly upon her. She finished at the office on Wednesday and handed over the keys of her flat to the new tenant, not without a twinge of regret, for she had had fun fitting the place up and feeling she was making a home. There wouldn't be a home to make in Hong

Kong. And afterwards—when they returned to England—well, she didn't dare look as far ahead as that.

On Thursday James and Catriona arrived from Edinburgh, with their two little daughters, and later that day Mr Webster drove to Heathrow to collect Ian and Joyce, after their long flight from New Zealand.

After that the old house was bursting at the seams, and Maggie was surrounded by a happy, excited, loving family, all chattering together, exchanging news, avid to know all about Blake, and about their plans. It was impossible to get a moment to herself, and as she still had one or two letters to deal with, left over from the office work, she carried her portable typewriter down to the little summerhouse hidden away among the pine trees in the wild part of the big, sprawling garden, and issued instructions that she wasn't to be disturbed unless the house was burning down.

Blake phoned late on Thursday afternoon to say he had just got back from New York. He sounded tired and slightly irritable. 'How did everything go?' Maggie asked him. After all, she couldn't expect him to enquire lovingly after her, or say he had missed her, could she?

'Pretty gruelling, it was like stepping into an oven every time you went out into the street. And I had a hell of a wrangle with Smith. I'm not sure we shouldn't consider someone else for the air-conditioning, Maggie. We haven't signed anything yet, have we, and I get a nasty feeling he's going to be a sticky customer to deal with. We'll discuss it when I see you.'

'And when will that be?' Maggie enquired quietly. What an odd conversation to have with one's husband-to-be just two days before the wedding!

'I'll try and make it early on tomorrow,' Blake said.

'Dad tells me you've already packed up at the office, so I'll come out to Amersham. There are one or two things I want to talk to you about—did you get the shipping order fixed up for the steel window-frames?'

Maggie sighed. 'Yes, Blake, I did. I've also had my wedding dress delivered and the cake has come. On top of that the whole of my family is now in residence, and although I love them dearly I'm afraid we shan't have much of an opportunity to talk business, if that's what you have in mind.'

He actually laughed at that. 'O.K., I get the point,' he said. 'We'll have to cut out the business part then and behave like two young lovers, shall we?'

She laughed too, although it was rather an effort. 'Will it be so very difficult for you?'

'Oh, I've no doubt we can put on a good show if we both try hard.'

Maggie felt like howling, but she kept her voice steady and said, 'I'll see you tomorrow, then, Blake. Are you quite sure it's convenient to come out here?'

He didn't seem to sense any irony in the remark. 'Oh, I think I can fit it in,' he said carelessly. 'If not, I'll give you a ring and you can come into town, can't you?'

'I expect so,' she said coolly. 'Goodbye, then, Blake.' She fumbled the receiver on to its stand, not trusting herself to continue the conversation. There were tears in her eyes, but she forced them back. It was *stupid*, she told herself fiercely, to care so much about how he spoke to her, but just hearing his deep voice brought all her love for him welling up inside her and with it a sense of utter frustration and a hollow fear that he would never love her.

Catriona came into the hall then, followed closely by her two small daughters, dark and pretty in their swinging kilts and white blouses, and refreshingly well behaved. 'We still understand the meaning of the word discipline up in the North,' James had grinned last night when the girls had gone off to bed with hardly a protest. 'Catriona's marvellous with them.'

Jessie, nine years old, and the elder by eighteen months, ran up to Maggie as she put the telephone down. 'Were you talking sweet nothings to your boyfriend, Auntie Maggie?'

Catriona's eyes met Maggie's apologetically. 'Where *do* they pick these expressions up?'

Jean, the seven-year-old, piped up, 'We found it in a book in the attic, and it said that the two lovers exchanged sweet nothings.'

'It sounds like a fairly antiquated book,' laughed the practical no-nonsense Catriona, but Maggie thought privately that 'nothings' exprssed quite well what she and Blake had just been exchanging. 'Nothings', but not particularly 'sweet'.

She was finding it increasingly difficult to talk about Blake to her family, but she felt that something was required of her now. 'Blake has just come home from the U.S.,' she volunteered. 'He sounded absolutely whacked, but I expect he'll be coming along tomorrow morning and then you can all meet him.'

'That will be grand,' said Catriona, smoothing down Jean's silky dark hair. 'We've heard so much about him from Gran, haven't we, girls?'

'Will he like my pink dress?' Jean enquired perkily.

Her sister stuck out her tongue. 'Silly, he won't be looking at you. He'll have no eyes for anyone but his bride as she walks up the aisle. It said so in that book too.'

'Don't put out your tongue, Jessie, it's very rude,'

Catriona reproved her elder daughter. 'And I think I shall have to supervise your reading matter more carefully, my girls. You're a little too young for romance!' But there was a twinkle in the goodhumoured grey eyes.

Jean was jumping up and down, her kilt flapping against her skinny little legs. 'Can I put on my pink dress now to show Auntie Maggie?'

'No,' her mother told her firmly. 'I've told you, not until tomorrow. I have to press it first. Now run off into the garden, both of you.'

Jean looked downcast and Maggie snatched her up in her arms and hugged her tightly. 'I'll look forward to seeing your dress tomorrow, poppet, and I'm sure you're going to look *smashing*, both of you!'

She watched the two little girls run out of the front door and across the lawn to where the men were just beginning to unpack the large marquee for the reception on Saturday. 'You've got two gorgeous children, Catriona,' she sighed, and the older girl looked keenly at her.

'You want a family, Maggie?'

Maggie felt the heat rise into her cheeks. 'There's nothing I'd like better.' Blake's children—little boys with Blake's long-lashed eyes and unruly dark hair. She felt weak at the thought.

'And Blake—does he want it too? Some men don't, I know, these days,' Catriona added unemotionally.

'Oh, I—we haven't discussed it yet,' Maggie said awkwardly.

Catriona shot her a quick glance but didn't press the subject. 'And where is the honeymoon to be? Or is that a closely-guarded secret?'

'Oh no, not at all. We're not having a proper honeymoon until later on. We're flying out to Hong Kong straight after the wedding, to get on with the job there, and we'll take time off when we can.' Maggie was improvising wildly. Blake hadn't even mentioned a honeymoon, which she supposed was understandable under the circumstances.

Her sister-in-law looked at her rather doubtfully. 'Is that a good idea, do you think? Honeymoons aren't always what they're cracked up to be, I know, but you do need time to adjust to each other.'

Maggie laughed a little selfconsciously. 'Oh, I think we've adjusted pretty well already. Blake and I have been working together for the last two years, you know.'

She met Catriona's quizzical glance and flushed crimson as she realised just what she had implied, but her sister-in-law merely smiled and said nothing.

'And of course,' Maggie rushed on nervously, 'it will be like a holiday, in a way, all so new and thrilling. I can't wait to see Hong Kong. It sounds a fabulous place.'

Catriona was an extremely intelligent young woman, with a disconcerting ability to read between the lines, and Maggie had a horrible feeling that she could somehow guess at the turmoil that was going on inside her at present. It was a relief when Ian and Joyce came downstairs just then, having been hustled up to bed by Mrs Webster a couple of hours ago, to sleep off their jet-lag.

Maggie loved all three of her brothers, but she and Ian had always been particularly close, especially as the two older boys usually paired off. Seeing him again was a special delight. He looked splendid, she thought, bronzed and fit, with the brown eyes and curly light brown hair so like her own. And he had broadened out quite noticeably; marriage evidently suited him.

It would be fun, too, to get to know Joyce better; they had only met once before, when Ian brought his new wife over for a very short stay soon after they were married. Joyce, slim and flaxen-haired and blue-eyed, was obviously a little shy among all these people whom she didn't know very well, and Maggie made a special effort to put her at ease and make her feel at home during supper and the rest of the evening, so she had no time to worry about her own fears and uncertainties.

But when Ian put a brotherly arm round her shoulder as she went up the stairs to bed and said softly, 'Well done, Sis, I'm glad you're taking the plunge. I can recommend marriage,' the tears were suddenly back in her eyes and she had to dash them away and smile.

'Tears of happiness—you know.'

Ian planted a kiss on her wet cheek. 'I know the score, little one,' he said softly in her ear, and pushed her gently up the stairs.

No girl, thought Maggie, as she closed her bedroom door, had ever had a happier childhood or a nicer, warmer family, and they were all living proof that marriages *can* work out happily. If only, she thought wistfully, I can somehow make mine go the same way!

After breakfast next morning Mrs Webster announced that she was taking them all to the church, to help arrange the flowers. She herself had been up at the crack of dawn, raiding the garden, and the big cool larder was full of buckets brimming over with tall spikes of delphiniums and lupins and special snow-white daisy-like flowers that had always grown to profusion in the garden and reminded Maggie of all the summer holidays and tennis parties and teas-under-the-apple-tree that had been the high spots of her childhood.

'Will you come with us, Maggie?' her mother asked,

and then, with a quick look at her daughter's pale face, 'Are you feeling all right, dear? Not been overdoing things?'

Maggie shook her head. 'I'm fine,' she lied. Actually, she was feeling more and more tense all the time. 'But I think I'll stay, because Blake said he'd probably come here this morning, and if he doesn't he'll phone.'

Her mother nodded sagely. 'You'll feel better when you've seen him. You've missed him these last few days, *I* know. Well, we'll all be off, and then you can have the place to yourselves when he arrives. Bring him down to the church later on, perhaps?'

'Yes, of course,' Maggie said brightly, and waved them all away in two cars filled with flowers and chattering, happy people. Guiltily, she felt a sense of relief when they had gone.

Alone in the house, she wandered about from room to room. There were still thank-you letters to be written, but she could settle to nothing until she had seen Blake. If he weren't able to come here, she decided, she would get into the Mini and drive into town to see him. Until she had spoken to him again she couldn't believe that all this—the flowers, the presents, the big white marquee on the lawn outside—was real. Even her own reflection as she caught sight of herself in mirrors as she passed them had the appearance of a small ghost in a pale green dress. She went up to her bedroom and changed into jeans and a red tee-shirt and dabbed her cheeks with blusher, something she normally used only in the evenings.

The phone rang twice and each time she dived to answer it. Once it was the caterers, asking questions about wine glasses. The other time a friend of Mrs Webster's to offer apologies for missing the wedding tomorrow, as her daughter's baby had to go into hospital. Maggie answered mechanically, hurrying through the calls in case Blake was waiting to get on the line.

When she hadn't heard from him by eleven o'clock she put a call through to the office. His secretary said he had been in and gone out again, he hadn't said where.

The phone rang again and this time it *was* Blake. He cut off her greeting abruptly with, 'Look, Maggie, I'm ringing from a phone box in the village. Are your family around just now?'

'No,' she said, slightly bewildered, 'they're all down at the church doing the flowers. Why?'

'I have to see you alone,' he said. 'Is that possible if I come to the house, or will you come down to the village?'

'There's no one here at all,' she said. 'But——?'

He cut her off. 'I'll see you in a few minutes,' he said. Maggie held the aimlessly clacking receiver away from her ear and stared at it. If most bridegrooms had said, 'I must see you alone,' it would be perfectly understandable, but the urgency she had heard in Blake's voice was of quite a different nature. Different, and vaguely alarming. Slowly she replaced the receiver and went to the front door to wait for him.

As soon as he got out of the car she saw from his face that something ominous had happened. He looked terrible. His eyes were black smudges and his cheeks below them were shadowy hollows. He was holding a folded newspaper, one of the tabloids, and as they went into the house he held it out to her without a word.

Splashed in banner headlines over half the front page were the words, DEATH OF A HERO, and underneath,

RACING DRIVER PIETRO MATTIOLI GIVES LIFE FOR RIVAL.

Her eyes went to the picture below. A crash on a racing circuit—two mangled cars ablaze—a man in racing suit stumbling across the track, half hidden in smoke and flame——

The newspaper dropped from her hand. 'I hadn't heard the news,' she faltered. 'How terrible! It was——'

He said heavily, 'The man Fiona married.' Then his voice quickened, became almost eager. 'She came to me last night, Maggie, she hadn't anyone else to turn to. She's in a dreadful state. She's at my flat now, I've been with her all night, trying to——' he shrugged '—to give her some comfort. They've only been married a bit over a month.'

He moved restlessly across to the hall window and stood with his back to her. Maggie stayed where she was. She felt as if the whole of her had been suddenly turned to stone. Her body, her brain, nothing was functioning, and all she was conscious of was a terrifying feeling of impending disaster that loomed ahead like a high, blank wall.

Blake swung round abruptly. 'Maggie, I can't go through with it,' he said.

'With—with what?' she faltered, but she knew what he was going to say.

'With this charade of a wedding tomorrow. I couldn't—not when Fiona needs me so badly.'

Maggie's knees sagged and she sank into the nearest chair. 'Can't you?' she said stupidly.

He came and stood over her, leaning forward, speaking urgently, the way he always spoke when he was trying to convince her of something, and expecting her to understand and agree with him. 'Of course I can't.

Don't you see, Maggie, it would be a sort of crime—a dishonesty.'

'Would it?'

'Of course it would!' He sounded angry, as if she were being purposely dimwitted.

'You still love her?' Maggie said dully. 'You want to marry her?'

He shrugged impatiently. 'That's all in the future. The point is that I couldn't possibly marry anyone else, now that Fiona is free. You do see that, don't you, Maggie?'

She put a hand on her forehead. 'I'm trying to. I can't quite—quite take it in yet. I—I don't see how we can just—cancel everything.'

She looked vaguely through the doorway into the big dining room, the table loaded with presents, the mantelpiece stacked with letters and cards.

'We've got to,' Blake said grimly. 'There's no other way.'

She stared at him. This wasn't Blake and herself; it couldn't be. It must be happening to two other people, or she was having a nightmare. 'You mean you'd just—walk out on me? Would you do that to me, Blake? It would be very—very humiliating.' Her voice was shaking so much she could hardly get the words out. Her teeth were chattering and she pressed her hand against her lips.

He said irritably, 'No, of course I wouldn't walk out on you. I couldn't do that to you after you've been so——' his mouth turned down wryly '—so accommodating about this whole business all along.'

There was the sound of a car approaching up the drive. The family was returning. Maggie was somehow galvanised into action. She grabbed Blake's arm and hurried him across the drawing-room and through the french window. Down the garden, past the big marquee and beyond the high hedge to the little summerhouse among the pine trees.

'We won't be interrupted here,' she said. She sank down on a wooden bench and waited numbly for him to speak.

He was silent for what seemed ages, sitting beside her, leaning forward, hands on knees, his face dark. At last he said moodily, 'This is all hellishly difficult, Maggie. If only I'd waited and not rushed into this crazy arrangement with you——'

'But you didn't wait,' she pointed out. If she could somehow manage to control her feelings and keep everything on a down-to-earth level there might be some hope. Blake had said he wouldn't let her down. She must cling on to that.

He said heavily, 'There's only one way out that I can see. I can't and won't walk out on you.'

The wave of relief almost threatened to drown her.

'So——' she began, fixing her eyes on him, willing him to say that the wedding must go on.

He met her look implacably. His dark eyes were narrowed in determination.

'So,' said Blake, '*you* must walk out on *me*.'

CHAPTER THREE

Maggie's hands closed convulsively over the edges of the wooden seat. She was getting colder and colder. Soon, her whole body would be numb, and that would be good because then she wouldn't be able to feel anything more. 'I'm not sure,' she said carefully, 'that I know what you mean.'

'It's the only way,' he said again, his voice rough. I've been thinking about it all night—trying to find some way out that wouldn't do too much damage.'

'That's very civil of you.' She was unable to keep the bitterness out of her voice. She didn't remind him that he had said he had spent the night comforting Fiona.

He turned to her quickly. 'Ah, don't be like that, Maggie, it's not like you. We've got to work this thing out together sensibly, otherwise we're all going to be sunk.'

'What did you have in mind, exactly?' It was strange how ordinary you could sound when you are frozen inside.

He got up restlessly and stood leaning against the wooden doorpost. She had the impression that he was trying to find the right words, which was unusual for Blake, who was normally so articulate. At last he swung round and said quickly, 'I think the best way is to let everything go on as planned, up to the ceremony itself. Then, when the moment arrives for you to walk up the aisle you—simply don't appear. In other words, you leave me standing at the altar.'

There was a silence, then Maggie said tightly, 'I see. Wouldn't that be a bit corny—like an old music-hall joke?'

He moved his hands impatiently. 'Can you think of anything better?'

'Yes,' Maggie said immediately, 'I can. We could go through with the marriage and then, quite soon, we could get an annulment.' If they were married, she thought desperately, there might be some faint hope for her. Blake might find he liked being married to her, that it suited him to have her with him on the job too well to let her go—Fiona might find another man—oh, anything might happen. But this horrible way that he was suggesting made her feel cheap, unclean almost.

'No,' he said sharply, 'I won't agree to that.'

She looked at the dark, arrogant face and thought she almost hated him. How could you hate someone and love them at the same time? She said, 'You're asking me to behave badly. Why can't *you* take the rap yourself?'

'Several reasons,' he said. 'One being that it would be the end of my career with the company. My father would never forgive me, he's very strict about things like that.'

'You'd have Fiona. Does your career matter more than her?'

He gave her an angry look. 'Don't be purposely obtuse, Maggie. You know bloody well how much my job means to me.'

'You want everything, don't you?' she said bleakly.

He brushed that aside. 'There's only one way out, for you to do the letting down, as I said. It would be easy for you—nothing would hang on it. It may still be a man's world, but the general feeling is that if a man lets a girl down he's a swine. But if the girl changes her mind nobody thinks any the worse of her for it. And if we do it my way there won't be any doubt about who's jilting whom.' He pulled a wry face. 'I don't say it's going to be particularly pleasant for me to stand at the altar, waiting for a bride who leaves me flat, but I'll have to accept that.'

'Seeing that it's all your idea, that's the least you can do,' said Maggie, with sudden asperity.

He glanced quickly at her. 'Exactly,' he said.

There was another long silence. Then Maggie said, 'And what about the job? What about Hong Kong?'

'That won't suffer. I'll fly out tomorrow evening, as arranged. Everyone will no doubt sympathise and understand that in the circumstances I want to get out of England as soon as possible. Fiona will join me later out there.'

'You've got it all fixed up nice and tidy, haven't you?'

He met her eyes and looked away, running a hand almost desperately through his hair. 'It's the only way. First things have to come first.'

'The first thing, of course, being that you must be free to marry Fiona?'

'Yes,' he said, 'that's exactly how it is.' He sat down beside her again. 'I knew you'd see it my way, Maggie.'

She ignored that. 'And what plans have you made for me? I take it you've worked that out as well?'

'Of course.' He felt in his pocket and drew out an envelope. 'Air travel ticket to Majorca, complete with hotel booking there for a fortnight. At my expense, of course. You can have a fortnight in the sun and then, when it's all blown over, you can come back and go on where you left off.'

'Can I? Are you sure? I don't imagine J.M. will want to keep me on in the company after this.'

'My dear Maggie, of course he will. My father thinks the world of you, and a girl can't be blamed for changing her mind. It'll all work out, you'll see,' he said eagerly. 'In eighteen months or so, when I get home from H.K., everything will be as it was before.'

'Nothing is ever as it was before,' said Maggie slowly.

He put a hand over hers and she had to steel herself not to pull away. 'I'm desperately sorry, Maggie, you must believe that. It's all a wretched mess and I'm to blame for letting you in for it. But it might be worse. It isn't as if our——' he smiled crookedly '—our deeper feelings were involved. And you've known the score, right from the start, I haven't kept anything from you. You knew I was crazy about Fiona.'

She said tautly, 'It's just a pity she wasn't crazy about you. That would have saved a lot of trouble.'

He said, 'She's very young. She was dazzled by the glamour and excitement of the motor-racing world. She admits that now.'

'Does she?' said Maggie dryly.

She saw his jaw set and knew he wouldn't discuss Fiona any further. After a moment she said, 'It's going to hurt my family terribly. All the preparations and the work—and my mother's been so happy arranging everything——'

He groaned. 'Yes, I know, I know, I wish to goodness I'd never agreed to a slap-up wedding in the first place. It was you who wanted it, not me. I'd much rather have had a quiet register office ceremony.'

Maggie said quietly, 'Your father was keen on it, as well as my people, if you remember.'

Blake shrugged. 'Oh well——! Of course you'll explain everything to them later, and tell them the whole story. I'm not asking you to cover up for me. It's only the short-term problem that we've got to solve, and a quick, clean cut is the best way.'

'So,' said Maggie, wondering how much longer she was going to be able to continue this conversation, 'the plan is for me to creep out of the house and drive myself to the airport tomorrow morning. I suppose I leave a note? As if I were committing suicide?'

He winced. 'You know how to hurt, don't you, Maggie?'

'I'm merely trying to be objective, that's what you want, isn't it? You wouldn't like me to lapse into hysterics and plead with you, I'm sure.' If you only knew, she thought frantically, how very near I am to doing just that!

A faint smile pulled at his mouth. 'That doesn't sound very like my Maggie.'

Your Maggie! she almost screamed. But instead she said quietly, 'You know me so well, don't you, Blake? You know what I'll think and feel, how I'll react?'

He glanced sharply at her, but her face was as calm as ever. 'Well, as much as anyone can know anyone else—yes, I think I do know you. Unlike many women you think clearly and reasonably. I knew I could rely on your good sense over this wretched business.' There was a touch of complacency in his voice now. He was sure he had convinced her.

The first part of this nightmare was nearly over now, she told herself, which was as well, because she couldn't stand much more.

Blake got to his feet and stood looking down at her. 'Thank you for being so understanding, Maggie. I'll never forget it.' He leaned forward and kissed her briefly on her cold lips.

She drew back, shuddering inwardly, as her mother's voice came across the garden. 'Maggie, are you there? Can you come to the phone, dear? It's Christine Baker and she'd like to speak to you.'

'Coming!' Maggie called back.

Blake looked over his shoulder apprehensively. 'I'll go out by the garden gate—I left my car in the lane.' He hesitated a moment and then took her hands and squeezed them hard. 'Bless you, Maggie, I'm fathoms deep in your debt.' He turned and escaped between the pine trees—back to Fiona, of course.

She didn't wait to see him go.

At six o'clock on that overcast July evening the old summerhouse was very quiet under its canopy of tall, dark trees. The nostalgic scent of pines, mingled with damp earth, came to Maggie as she sat alone at the wooden table, trying to compose the note that seemed to her like a death warrant.

After Blake had left this morning she had moved through the events of the day like a zombie, her limbs heavy as lead, her head aching dully, and a sick feeling in the pit of her stomach.

She had said what had to be said: 'Blake was so sorry he missed you all,' and: 'It was really too bad, but he simply *had* to rush back to the office to tidy up a lot of loose ends,' and other explanations that sounded feeble in the extreme to her. But everyone accepted them without question. Everyone except, possibly, Catriona, and if she had any doubts she kept them to herself.

Somehow Maggie got through lunch. After lunch she played with the children in the garden, in and out of the marquee; that was easier. Later in the afternoon Miss Parsons, her mother's visiting hairdresser, arrived to do her hair, and after that the rest of the evening stretched ahead emptily.

It would have been better if she had had something to busy herself with. But her mother had organised everything, down to the last detail. The wedding dress hung, swathed in tissue, in her room. Her going-away case was packed except for a few last-minute items that might crush. The little brown and cream suit she was to wear for the journey hung in the wardrobe, together with hand baggage she would take with her into the plane.

But here in the summerhouse, another travelling bag was packed, and hidden behind the stack of deck-chairs in a corner, together with a pair of corduroy trousers, a light top, and a jacket, all ready for a different journey.

And now she sat at the wooden table, her typewriter pushed aside, gripping her pen in nerveless fingers. The note must be in her own handwriting, and she must somehow put her unhappiness into it, so that they might understand a little and perhaps forgive her.

She began, 'Dear Everyone——' Then her eye fell on the corner of her travelling bag, sticking out from behind the stack of chairs. Glancing over her shoulder, her heart racing, she jumped up and pushed it out of sight. This must be what it felt like to plan a murder, she thought ghoulishly.

In fact, the planning hadn't been difficult. Part of her brain seemed, miraculously, to be working much as usual. 'You think clearly and reasonably,' Blake had told her. Well, that was lucky for him, wasn't it?

She rehearsed the scene again as if it were in a play. She could see it all in her mind quite clearly. Time: to-morrow morning. Place: the hall of the house. The wedding party would have just left for the church and she would be alone with her father. Daddy would be all dressed up in his morning suit with the cream rosebud in his buttonhole. She would be in her silky ivory lace, with the coronet of pearls and the filmy veil that floated down over her curly brown hair.

She would suddenly seem to remember and say, 'Daddy, wait here for me, there's something I want in the summerhouse. You know—you're supposed to wear "something old, something new, something borrowed, something blue" and I've got a yen to take a little blue brooch I hid down there ages ago, when I was about ten. It'll be lucky.'

Daddy would look anxiously at the flowing ivory lace and say, 'You'll mess up your dress and your mother will never forgive me. Couldn't I get it for you, sweetheart?'

'You wouldn't know where it's hidden,' she would say airily, 'I'm not quite sure myself. No, you wait here for me, I won't be a minute.'

Then the quick flight down the garden, past the marquee, with the waitresses gathered round the entrance, goggling at the sight of the flying bride. Under the pine trees into the summerhouse. Strip off and into trousers and top. Place note prominently on heap of white lace on floor, pick up travelling bag. Through the trees to the Mini, standing alone in the garage, and off along the road to the West. (Blake had been clever not to book a flight from Heathrow or Gatwick. That would be where they would look first. They'd never think of Bristol.) At airport, leave Mini in long-stay car park and mix with the crowd. Check in—passport control—departure lounge—final flight call—board plane. Then airborne to—— what? She wouldn't think about that yet.

Oh yes, it was all well planned. Like a perfect crime. And in a way it was a crime, she thought, passing a hand over her aching forehead.

She began again on the note. 'Dear Everyone, Please try to forgive me, but I can't go through with this wedding. I'll come back soon and explain everything. I know how much this will hurt you, but believe me, it has to be done this way. *Please, please* forgive and don't hate me. Your ever loving and most unhappy, Maggie.'

She sealed the envelope and pushed it into the top of

her travelling bag, hidden behind the chairs. There, it was done!

Outside the summerhouse there was a crackle of twigs on the carpet of pine-needles and she spun round to see Jean standing in the doorway in her pink bridesmaid's dress, her small face a picture of triumph and apprehension. 'Auntie Maggie, Mummy said I shouldn't come down here and please don't be cross, but I wanted you to see my dress,' she gabbled excitedly, and performed a pirouette, her arms held wide.

Maggie had no time to respond, for Catriona appeared then, flushed and agitated, with Jessie tagging along after her, also in her bridesmaid's array.

'You naughty girl!' Catriona scolded her youngest. 'You know quite well Auntie Maggie isn't to be disturbed when she's in the summerhouse.' She turned apologetically to Maggie. 'I'm so sorry, Maggie. Jean got away from me while I was fixing Jessie's dress. They should have waited until you came in, but they're overexcited, I'm afraid. Come along, girls, and leave Auntie Maggie to finish her letters.'

'No, let them stay,' Maggie pleaded as she saw Jean's lower lip begin to protrude pathetically. 'I've finished my letters anyway. I was just coming up to the house. Now, let me look at your dresses. My goodness, you do look splendid! Like two little sugared almonds.'

The little girls giggled, delighted, and Maggie turned to their mother. 'The dresses are super, Catriona. You didn't make them yourself, surely?' Catriona was known to be a very clever dressmaker. 'All that lovely embroidery on the collars—and the smocking on the bodices! It must have taken hours and hours.'

Catriona nodded, smiling with pleasure. 'It was a labour of love. I enjoyed doing it, and the girls have been so thrilled. They've lived for nothing else for weeks, ever since they knew about the wedding. It's their very first wedding—and it's so lovely that it's in the family. They'll remember it all their lives.' Her pleasant face became serious. 'First impressions are so important at their age and I believe that they'll grow up thinking of marriage as something lovely and worth-while—which is a blessing in these casual days.'

Maggie could say nothing. There was a huge lump in her throat as she looked at the two little girls, who were going to have a very different memory of their first wedding.

Jessie pulled at her hand. 'Aunt Maggie, please can we have a re-hearsal?' She brought out the long word carefully. She led Maggie into the little clearing outside the summerhouse. 'Let's pretend this is the church and we're walking behind you.' Two large pairs of eyes gazed hopefully up at her.

Maggie walked slowly the length of the clearing and turned to see the pair following solemnly, hand in hand, their pink dresses vivid against the darkness of the trees.

Her breath suddenly caught in her throat. 'Darlings, you do it beautifully,' she told them unsteadily. 'Now, go along with Mummy and take off those pretty dresses. Until tomorrow.'

Her eyes, swimming in tears, met Catriona's, who smiled back sympathetically. 'Nervous, dear? But it'll be all right on the day, you'll see.' She smiled encouragingly and shepherded her daughters back towards the house.

Maggie stood very still, her face stony. It wouldn't be all right on the day. It would be terribly wrong for everyone—including those two little girls, who would remember their first experience of a wedding as a day of disappointment and bewildered unhappiness.

She stood there for what seemed an age, motionless. Then she said aloud. 'There *must* be a better way. There *must*!'

Galvanised into action, she turned and ran towards the garage.

Joe, the local jobbing gardener, was there, polishing up the family car ready for tomorrow. Her mother's Mini was standing outside the garage. 'I have to dash into Town, Joe. Would you mind letting someone know in the house, please? Say I won't be long, I'll be back in time for supper.'

'Right you are, Miss Maggie.' Joe stopped polishing. 'She's coming up a treat, isn't she?' He stood away from the glossy dark-green Humber, shaking out his polishing cloth. 'Do you proud tomorrow, Miss Maggie.'

'Yes, indeed, the car looks super, Joe. You've done a grand job.' Maggie smiled at the elderly man as she climbed into the Mini. Everything was geared to the wedding. Everyone was working for it, loking forward to it. She started up the engine and let in the clutch clumsily—unusual for Maggie, who was a good, safe driver. As the little car jerked forward she thought fiercely. He shan't hurt and disappoint them all like this. I'll make him see that he must think of some other way.

Driving into London at this time in the evening was marginally easier than driving out of it, but even so it took Maggie over an hour to reach Blake's apartment overlooking the river.

When she had been here before she had never felt particularly attracted to the place, with its atmosphere of almost suffocating luxury, but now she wasn't noticing the surroundings as she pressed Blake's number on the board in the lobby.

'Who's that?' came a woman's languid voice through the speaker.

Fiona! Maggie's heart sank. Stupid of her—she'd been so bent on talking to Blake that she hadn't given a thought to the certainty that Fiona would still be here. Oh well, she had to go through with it now.

'It's Maggie Webster. I'd like to see Blake, please.'

'Oh!' A pause. Then, 'You'd better come up,' said Fiona.

Maggie was sucked silently up in the lift. She wielded the tiny ornate brass knocker on the white door and a voice from inside said, 'Come in, it's not locked.'

Fiona was stretched out on a satin-pillowed divan in the long living-room that had a magnificent view of the river from its picture windows. She was pale and she looked, Maggie had to admit, fabulously beautiful in her clinging black negligee, her silver-gilt hair loose around her shoulders. She made no attempt to rise and Maggie stood looking down at her. Some words of sympathy needed to be said, and she murmured. 'I was so sorry to hear of the tragedy. It must have been terrible for you.'

Fiona raised enormous sapphire-blue eyes. 'Oh— Pietro. Yes, it was too bad. He was leading in the race, too.' She sighed. 'All that prize lolly down the drain!' Her lovely mouth took on a petulant slant. 'He never told me he owed money all round Italy, would you believe? That was like Pietro—he was so *selfish*. He never gave a thought to what I should do if he got himself killed.' She shuddered delicately and swung her silken legs off the divan. 'I was lucky to get out of the country before I was clobbered for his debts, I suppose. Not that I could have paid them—I hadn't a bean.'

Maggie listened to this incredible speech in silent amazement, as Fiona reached for the glass on the low table beside her. 'Blake's quite different, of course. A solid businessman, is Blake, and he's consoling me beautifully.' Fiona glanced with a kind of tolerant contempt round the luxurious apartment.

She put down the glass, and her face suddenly became closed and suspicious. 'What do you want to see Blake about? He said he'd arranged everything with you about tomorrow.' She smiled again. 'Silly boy, rushing off and getting himself engaged to you when he found I'd got married, but he explained that it was just a business arrangement. So of course it's quite easy to cancel everything.'

Maggie stared at her. 'Is that how you see it?'

'Well, of course. Blake doesn't care two pins for you, my dear, you must know that. You're useful to him in his business, but he'll easily find someone else.'

Maggie dug her fingernails into her palms. To smack that lovely face would be satisfying but wouldn't help matters. She said, 'I'd like to see Blake. Do you know where he is?'

Fiona smiled. 'He's at his stufffy old office, busy with all his last-minute arrangements. He thinks he's flying to Hong Kong tomorrow.'

'*Thinks?*'

Fiona fingered a slender gold bracelet. 'Oh yes, darling, *thinks*. He doesn't know it yet, but he's not going to Hong Kong. It's not my favourite place. He's coming to Paris—with me. I shall be on the spot to console him——' she smiled silkily '—when the bride fails to turn up.'

She took another sip of her drink and nodded lazily towards the telephone. 'You won't want to trek over to the office this time of night. Ring him from here.'

'No, thanks,' Maggie said curtly. For a moment her

eyes studied the girl on the divan, taking in the beautiful body, the exquisite face, seeing under it all to the callous, mean, squalid little mind beneath. 'I don't think I really need see Blake, after all.'

Fiona shrugged. 'Suit yourself. Ta-ta then, darling.' She tossed off the remainder of her drink and giggled. 'I can't very well say I'll see you in church, can I?'

Maggie turned and walked out of the apartment without another word.

She stumbled down the stairs, not waiting to call the lift. She couldn't get away from Fiona Deering quickly enough; she felt as if she were escaping from someone with a fatally infectious disease.

Reaching the Mini, she climbed into the driving seat and sat there, shaking all over with nerves and pure rage and disgust. But after a few minutes she pulled her scattered wits together and tried to think clearly. If she drove to the office and saw Blake what could she say? What good would it do to try to open his eyes to the kind of woman Fiona was? None at all, reason told her. Blake was infatuated and wouldn't listen or believe.

What other course remained? For a moment her pulse quickened and her stomach was suddenly hollow as she realised what she had to do. Then her resolution hardened and her small, square chin firmed stubbornly.

Could she let that woman ruin Blake's career and bring unhappiness to his father and all her own beloved family? 'Over my dead body!' she ground out between her teeth, and the hand that went to the self-starter was firm and steady.

The rush-hour traffic had cleared and the drive home was fairly easy. Maggie left the Mini outside the garage and made her way through the trees to the summer-house. She took the travelling bag from its hiding place behind the stack of chairs and carried it swiftly up the garden towards the front door.

Her mother was passing through the hall as she opened the door. 'Darling, you *have* been ages. Joe said you had to drive into London to see Blake about something.' Mrs Webster's face held the expression it had held for ages—as if she were concentrating on keeping at least three things in her mind at once. 'Catriona's putting the girls to bed and they do so want you to go up and say goodnight. Oh, and supper's nearly ready.'

She looked enquiringly at the bag in Maggie's hand and then at the small, determined face that showed a heightened spot of colour on each cheek. 'Everything all right, dear?'

Maggie kissed her swiftly. 'Everything's fine. Just something I remembered I had to collect from Blake. I'll be down in a minute to help you with the supper.'

Up in her room she unpacked the bag and pushed the contents back into drawers and cupboards. She picked up the note, where it had fallen on the floor, and held it in her hand for a long moment—the note that would have changed the course of several people's lives.

Then, with firm resolve, she tore the envelope and its contents into shreds and dropped them into the waste basket.

Blake phoned soon after they had started supper. Her mother called her to the telephone in the hall and then tactfully returned to the dining room, closing the door behind her.

'I've just got back from the office,' Blake's voice sounded tired and strained. 'I hear you came to the apartment, Maggie. Was there something special you wanted to see me about?'

Maggie stared at the wall in front of her, unable to speak.

'Maggie—are you still there? Is anything wrong?' His voice had sharpened.

She swallowed. 'It wasn't anything important.'

'You're all right?'

Oh, yes, she thought wildly. I'm on top of the world, what did you expect? 'Quite all right,' she said levelly.

'Good. I just wondered—I thought you sounded——' he paused. 'Everything set for tomorrow according to plan?'

'Everything,' she said. Then, on a crazy impulse, she added, 'I simply can't wait, darling, I'm so living for the moment.'

There was an awkward little laugh from the other end of the line, then Blake said, 'I take it you're not alone?'

Maggie looked round the empty hall and laughed too, high and brittle. 'What do *you* think?' she said.

'Oh well, then, it's not much use continuing this conversation. Just so long as I'm sure you're all ready for the morning.' A heavy meaning lay across the words.

'All ready,' she told him brightly. 'No problems at all.'

There was a short silence, then Blake said with the utmost sincerity, 'You're a wonderful girl, Maggie, and a wonderful friend. I always knew I could rely on you.'

'Thank you, Blake.' She replaced the receiver very carefully, thinking that that was the last compliment she would receive from Blake for a long, long time. Probably the last in her whole life.

That night Maggie didn't sleep at all. The thought of

tomorrow, and of what she intended to do, sent her hot and cold by turns, until at one time in the small hours of the morning she wondered if she was really ill. That might solve a lot of problems. But by the time it was light she knew that she wasn't going to be let off as easily as that. Her physical symptoms were nothing more than a reaction to an almost intolerable stress.

At six o'clock she crept downstairs and put the kettle on. A couple of minutes later she was joined by Catriona, her long, sandy hair loose on her patterned kimono, her pleasant face pink from sleep.

'Hullo, Maggie, I heard you come down. We both had the same idea. A lovely cup of tea, don't you think?'

Just seeing the practical Catriona restored a semblance of normality to the nightmare world in which Maggie seemed to be existing. 'Oh *yes*, that would be a life-saver.'

Catriona made the tea and poured out two cups, scalding hot. 'Drink that, my dear, it'll steady you up. You're a bundle of nerves, I can see. The idea of the bride going to bed early and having a long, long sleep the night before the wedding has always seemed like wishful thinking to me. I didn't sleep a wink the night before my wedding—and as you know that wasn't a big church affair, like yours.'

She chatted on, but her eyes were watching Maggie's face closely, and as they stood up she leaned forward and kissed her, which was a rare gesture from the usually undemonstrative Catriona.

'Being married is sometimes heaven and occasionally the other place,' she said. 'If you ever need a friendly ear, Maggie, and no questions asked, you know where to find me. Now, I think I hear those two bairns of mine, I must go and quell them before they get over-excited.'

As the morning wore on Maggie thought bleakly that it would have been fitting if the weather had been cold and wet. Instead it was turning into a perfect summer day. 'Just the kind of day,' everyone said happily, 'that we would have chosen.' Warm and sunny, with a heat-haze rising over the lawn. Inside the big marquee the waitresses had arrived and were setting out the buffet tables. Inside the house the scent from the bowls of roses that were everywhere filled the air, together with an almost tangible atmosphere of excited expectancy, as the family gathered in its wedding attire. Outside on the gravel sweep the glossy cars waited.

In Maggie's room Mrs Webster was giving her daughter a final check-over before leaving in the family car with Ian and Joyce. Maggie stood at the foot of the bed, like a pale statue, the silky white lace shimmering round her slim body and falling in flutes to the carpet, the tulle veil floating out from the tiny pearl coronet that nestled among her brown curls.

Her mother stood back, scrutinising her with the critical eye of the artist and finally announced, 'Yes, dear, you look *very* nice. I've never seen you look prettier. A little pale, though. You don't think a touch of colour on your cheeks? No? Well, perhaps not.' She fussed for a moment with the veil, her eyes misty. 'Darling girl, I hope—I wish you everything that——' She choked, groped for a handkerchief and blew her nose. 'I was determined not to weep, and here I am already!'

She repaired the damage at Maggie's dressing table, taking peeks out of the window at the same time. 'Look, James and Catriona are just leaving with the girls. Don't they look simply adorable, with those dear little posies?

It's a tremendous occasion for them, they'll always remember their very first wedding. Well now, dear, it's time to go down, Daddy will be waiting for you in the hall.'

Ian was standing by the front door as Maggie followed her mother slowly down the stairs. 'Come along, Mum,' he urged. 'Joyce is in the car already.' He saw Maggie behind his mother and whistled with cheerful lack of solemnity. 'You look stunning, Sis! Good luck, and mind you don't fluff your lines!'

He hustled his mother out to the car and Maggie was alone in the hall with her father.

Outside, the hired Daimler stood waiting, the sunshine gleaming on its glossy bonnet with the discreet trim of white satin ribbons. Beside her was her father, so dear and infinitely reassuring, broad and good-looking in his well-fitting morning suit, his grey hair carefully parted, the usual half-teasing smile that had seen her through so many childhood difficulties firmly in place.

She remembered her careful plan of yesterday. This was the moment when she should be making her excuse and running down the garden to the summerhouse and then—into the Mini and driving furiously away from the wedding and everthing connected with it.

But all that had changed now. Fiona had finally changed it last night. The scenario was a different one.

Her father touched her arm gently. 'Well, chickabiddy—' that was his childish pet-name for her '—are you ready for the fray? Shall we go forth to battle together?'

To battle! He couldn't guess how terrifyingly close to the truth that might be.

She put her hand in the crook of his arm and smiled up into his quizzical face. Unlike her mother he never seemed to hurry and was always apparently unflappable. 'Let's go,' she said, and they went out together to the waiting car.

CHAPTER FOUR

THE church was a mere ten minutes' drive away, but they were the longest ten minutes of Maggie's life. She was going to stab Blake in the back, and she was sick with fear of what he would do, knowing how his anger could flare and blaze. But there was no turning back now; she had burned her boats and she had to take whatever came later.

In the porch Catriona was hovering over her two small daughters, patting the little wreaths of daisies on their brown hair while they squirmed and fidgeted, their shell-pink dresses fluttering against the background of grey stone walls, their eyes huge with excitement and awe.

Catriona sighed with relief as Maggie and her father walked up the wide path, between the two rows of passers-by who had gathered to see the bride arrive.

'Here you are, then, both of you,' she whispered, almost as if she had expected some last-minute hitch. 'You look absolutely smashing, love, a really beautiful bride.'

Maggie smiled remotely. In her shimmer of ivory lace, with the floating tulle veil and the trailing sheaf of rosebuds nestling against the feathery green fern, she knew she looked like a bride; her mirror had told her that before she left her bedroom. But she didn't feel like a bride, she felt like a criminal.

Catriona fussed over the bridesmaids, lining them up behind Maggie and her father. 'Now, don't forget, Jessie, to take Auntie Maggie's flowers when she turns and gives them to you. Jean, keep hold of Jessie's hand as you walk up the aisle, and don't look around you.'

In the doorway one of the ushers held up a finger and the organ stopped playing, signalling the arrival of the bride. An expectant hush passed over the congregation and Maggie shivered in the sudden silence.

'All set?' Catriona looked at Maggie.

It wasn't too late, she thought, panicking suddenly. She could turn and run—and run——

'All set,' she nodded, her fingers gripping her father's coat-sleeve, her knees trembling violently.

The organ music began to throb softly through the old, lofty building and the little procession moved slowly into the church.

Maggie willed her feet forward, her eyes cast down. She was oblivious to everything—the music, the scent of flowers, the heads that turned as she passed, the sunlight that filtered through the stained glass, throwing jewel colours on to the carpet. Only one blinding fact possessed her mind: that Blake was standing there at the chancel rails, and that he must be shocked and furious that the bride he had not expected and did not want was coming down the aisle to him.

As she took her place at his side she did not dare to look up. She was agonisingly aware of his tall, rigid form in the unaccustomed dark suit, of the way his hand clenched convulsively, the knuckles showing white against the taut, brown skin. She heard his harsh intake of breath, and panic almost overcame her. In a moment he would turn and stride away from her in disgust. She had a terrible certainty that he would.

The minister's voice reached her as if through a fog. 'Dearly beloved, we are gathered together here, in the sight of God, and in the face of this congregation, to join together this Man and this Woman——'

The ceremony continued. Only Maggie could hear the suppressed rage that kept Blake's voice strong and firm as he made the responses. Her own words were scarcely audible and once or twice she stumbled over them. The touch of Blake's hand on hers as he slipped the ring on to her finger was a kind of agony.

'Those whom God hath joined together let no man put asunder.'

Only then, with a supreme effort, Maggie lifted her eyes to Blake's face. He was staring straight ahead of him, his expression stern and fixed. His features might have been graven from stone. She swallowed a sob. She had married Blake against his will and already he had rejected her.

In the vestry Maggie signed her name 'Margaret Webster' for the last time. She watched Blake sign, saw him straighten up. This was the moment when, traditionally, the bride and groom kissed each other. His mouth twisted cynically before it came down to hers, his lips were hard and unyielding. Oh God, she thought in sick misery, what have I done? At least Blake had been her friend before, now he was her bitter enemy.

The organ burst out triumphantly and Maggie passed back down the aisle on her husband's arm, a smile fixed on her mouth. It was when they had nearly reached the church door that she saw Fiona, in one of the back pews on the groom's side of the church. She was dressed in scarlet with a tiny scarlet wisp of veiling over her shining white-gold hair. She was a widow of only a few days, but here she was wearing scarlet, the colour of triumph, not of mourning. Last night she had taunted Maggie, gloated over the fact that she would be on the spot to console Blake when he was left standing at the altar. In the event, she had witnessed his marriage to the woman she had sneered at.

For a split second, as Maggie passed by on her husband's arm, the eyes of the two girls met and Maggie saw the venomous hostility in Fiona's lovely, petulant face. It was Maggie's moment of triumph, but she couldn't savour it; she felt terrible.

'Come along, dears, the photographer is all ready.' Mrs Webster began to organise the various groups. Maggie walked outside into the sunlight, her arm still in Blake's, her heart down in her ivory satin shoes.

After that she remembered very little of her wedding. She had done what she had nerved herself to do and now she was in a state of suspended shock, where nothing outside really registered. She supposed she must have smiled and said all the right things, but she moved through the hours like a girl in a dream.

It was very warm inside the marquee in the garden. The smell of good food mingled with that of cut grass and the perfume of the women. The waitresses flitted round with their trays, champagne corks popped, the guests laughed and talked and always there was an admiring group around Blake and Maggie.

The cake was cut and handed around, speeches were made, Blake's the shortest and most conventional of them all. When he said, 'My wife and I——' Maggie winced inside as if she was some sort of impostor.

Mrs Webster moved happily among the crowd, basking in the success of her weeks of work and planning.

'Everything,' she whispered triumphantly to Maggie, as the reception began to draw to its inevitable close, 'has gone *splendidly*. And doesn't dear Blake look *super*? Such an exciting-looking man, and so *distinguished*! You're a lucky girl, Maggie darling.'

'Yes, aren't I?' said Maggie, smiling brilliantly.

'Who's the glamour-girl in red that Blake's talking to?' Mrs Webster's eyes went to the long white-clothed table, where the remains of the wedding cake still rose on its pillared silver platform, dark and moist. Blake was close to Fiona, their backs towards the assembled company. His head was bent towards her and he was talking earnestly.

'I—I don't think I know her,' Maggie faltered. 'Probably one of the family on Blake's side. His father invited so many people, I haven't met all of them yet.' She swallowed. 'Isn't it time I went up to change? We don't want to be late checking in for the plane.' She supposed they would still be flying to Hong Kong. At any rate, she would act as if they were, until Blake told her otherwise.

But he was waiting for her when she came downstairs from her bedroom. She wore the cream suit with the cinnamon piping which her mother had fallen in love with when they shopped together. Her curly brown hair was tidy, her face composed—and only she herself knew how much effort it was to keep it that way.

There were goodbyes to the immediate family. Mrs Webster was a little tearful now the moment of parting had come, Maggie's father a tower of strength, shaking hands with everyone. J.M. was there too, with a sister from Newcastle-on-Tyne. Maggie's brothers gathered around with their wives and the two little bridesmaids, flushed and tired but still exuberant.

The big hired Daimler that would drive the couple to the airport stood in the drive. As they went out the guests from the marquee swarmed around them, confetti fell in showers, Ian was working away suspiciously at the back of the car. It was a very conventional wedding.

'Goodbye—goodbye——' Maggie hugged her mother for the final time and climbed in. Blake followed. His father leaned in at the car door, his big, bluff face radiant. 'This is one of the happiest days of my life,' he told them. 'Ring me from Hong Kong, when you arrive.'

Blake nodded. 'I'll do that.' J.M. shook his hand, patted Maggie's arm and closed the car door. The Daimler moved slowly away down the drive, with Ian's cardboard 'Just Married' sign attached to its rear bumper.

Maggie sat back exhaustedly. She was so tired that she hardly cared what happened now, what Blake said.

It began almost before the car had left the drive and turned into the main road. Blake leaned deliberately towards Maggie, his eyes blazing savagely into hers.

'You damned treacherous little bitch!' he ground out between his teeth. 'I must have been bloody mad to think I could trust you. You're just a cheating, lying——' The horrible words poured out. He must have been holding back the torrent of anger all these hours, and now it erupted over Maggie like scalding lava from a volcano. On and on it went, as if he would never stop finding words that would stab and wound. She felt as if she were being pierced by sharp daggers and she put her hands over her ears, moaning, trying to shut out the pitiless onslaught, but he dragged them away, holding them in a merciless grip so that her arms twisted painfully.

'Don't,' she pleaded. 'Please don't—the driver——'

She looked desperately at the back of the uniform cap behind the glass screen.

Blake laughed nastily. 'He'll think I can't wait to get my hands on my new wife, and how right he is! I'd like to bloody well strangle you, you——' His hands were round her throat, his fingers digging into her soft flesh, his face, dark with rage, only inches from her own.

'Please——' Her own voice sounded a long way away, thin and shrill. Outside the car window the scene lurched crazily. Then everything blacked out. Maggie had fainted.

She opened her eyes. The car was still moving steadily among the traffic on the wide main road, the driver still sitting stolidly behind the wheel. Blake was chafing her cold hands, his face devoid of expression.

'Are you all right?' he said indifferently, as if he thought she had been shamming. He didn't speak her name.

She dragged herself up, one hand to the throat where it felt sore and bruised.

'Oh, I'm fine,' she croaked with a watery smile. 'You didn't quite manage to murder me. What headlines that would have made tomorrow morning. Bride strangled in wedding car. Quite a new gimmick!' Her voice rose hysterically.

'Shut up!' he rapped out. 'It's not funny.'

'I didn't think it was,' she said. 'But don't they say something about making the best of a bad job? We'll both have to practise, Blake. For a start, you might apologise for your disgusting attack on me just now.'

She groped in the pocket of her suit for a handkerchief and wiped her eyes. She had a hazy feeling that if she could avoid showing her shock and misery; if she could somehow manage to behave towards Blake as she had always done in the past, when they could tease each other and joke together, it might somehow make the immediate future more bearable.

'Apologise?' His mouth was a thin, bitter line. 'It's you who should apologise. My God!' His lip curled contemptuously. 'To think I trusted you—that I believed you when you promised to fall in with my plan. I was straight with you, why the hell did you have to be so tricky and devious? Why did you promise——?'

It was too much to take. 'I didn't promise,' she broke in.

'You didn't—what the blazes are you saying?' His eyes, hard and cold now that his first anger had expressed itself, accused her. 'Of course you promised. It was all arranged. It——'

'*You* arranged it all,' she pointed out reasonably. 'You just took it for granted I would do as you told me, just as I always had done when you were my boss. But you're not my boss any longer, Blake, you're my husband. And if you remember,' she went on steadily, 'I didn't promise to obey.'

He sat back in his seat, watching her. His grey eyes were hard now and cold and she saw that his temper had worked itself out. 'No,' he said. 'Women don't promise to obey these days, but I'm looking at one woman who *will* obey.'

'W-hat do you mean?'

'I mean,' he said, 'that I intend to extract every little bit of advantage out of the situation. You chose to marry me, so you'll have to take the consequences.'

She stared back at him, at the menace in the grey-green eyes, at the cruel line of his mouth, and it was like looking at a stranger.

Her mouth went dry. 'Don't you—don't you want to

know why I—why I acted as I did?' she stammered.

'Not particularly.' He tossed away the suggestion with contempt. 'I've got my own ideas about that, and you'd probably lie anyway.'

'I wouldn't,' she burst out. 'Indeed I wouldn't, Blake. I can explain what happened——'

But could she? Could she say, 'I found out how awful Fiona was and I couldn't bear to let you be taken in by her?' Or could she say, 'J.M. told me that you'd ruin your career if you married her?' Or 'I couldn't bear to disappoint my family?'

There was part of the truth in all those things, but in the end the explanation boiled down to one stark, simple fact that she could never tell him: 'Because I love you.'

She stared blindly out of the car window. 'Are you going to drop me off somewhere before we get to Heathrow?' she asked dully. 'I don't suppose you want me with you any longer.'

'Drop you off?' He spoke in a jeering voice she had never heard before. 'Not on your life, my girl. You don't get out of it as easily as that. You're coming to Hong Kong with me, as arranged. We're on our honeymoon— remember? I've booked us in at a quiet, old-fashioned hotel in Macao. Just the place for a honeymoon, they tell me, peaceful and off the beaten track. We'll have a long, wonderful weekend there before we go across to Hong Kong Island and start on the job. Don't you think that's a lovely idea, darling little wife?'

She bit her lip. 'I—I don't know what to say. I feel I don't know you, Blake, not when you're like this.'

His lips curled. 'Too true you don't know me! You've got a lot to learn, my dear Maggie. I hope you're going to enjoy it. Now, suppose we consider the conversation closed. I've no wish to spend the flight making light conversation.' He leaned back and shut his eyes.

There was certainly no light conversation on the long, tedious journey. In fact, there was nothing that could be called conversation at all. Blake took charge of everything—checking in, tickets, luggage, passports. He strode through the busy terminal at Heathrow with an air of insolent arrogance that had the effect of making the less assured passengers move out of his way, so that he jumped queues shamelessly. Maggie watched him with a burning love-hate emotion and tagged along behind. Back to square one, she told herself with a feeble attempt at humour, and me being Blake's poodle, following obediently after the Great Man. At the moment she was too exhausted, physically and emotionally, to do anything else, but once they arrived, she promised herself, it would all be different.

Somehow the hours passed. She leafed through the magazines that Blake had tossed into her lap when they took their seats on the plane. She pretended to sleep most of the time, because when her eyes were closed she didn't have to see Blake's profile, hard and grim, his head bent over the papers he had taken from his briefcase and spread out on the table in front of his seat. Most of the time he ignored her completely, except when meals were served, and then he treated her to the minimum of attention.

He wasn't rude, he was ice-cold now, which was almost worse. Maggie began to feel like a criminal who was being escorted to some foreign prison. In spite of his furious threats, she couldn't believe that Blake really intended to harm her when they reached their destination, but little wriggles of fear became more and more frequent as the long hours dragged past.

Twenty hours flying time (it felt more like twenty years), then a taxi-ride through colourful, crowded streets enclosed by high buildings, through a tunnel and out again within sight of the busy harbour she had glimpsed when the plane came down to land.

The taxi took them to what looked like a quay or landing stage. Blake paid the driver and turned to Maggie. 'We get a jetfoil from here to Macao,' he said shortly, speaking directly to her for the first time for hours. 'You wait here with the luggage and I'll see what I can book.'

Maggie stood obediently beside their travelling cases. It was very, very hot, with a humid heat that seeped straight through her light suit, leaving her skin damp and clammy. Her head was aching and she felt confused and tired to the point of collapse.

When a man's voice, vaguely familiar, came from behind she started violently. 'Maggie—my dear girl, but what a lucky chance that we should meet so soon! When did you arrive, and where's your new husband? I was devastated that I couldn't make it to your wedding. J.M. cabled me an invitation, but I was in the wilds of Mexico.'

Maggie blinked against the dazzle of the sun on the blue water and saw the pleasant face of Nicholas Grant, the Corporation's consultant architect. 'Nick—how lovely! I never dreamed of meeting up with you here.' She felt a quick rush of relief, after the hours of strain and silence between herself and Blake.

They stood on the quayside, with the heat burning down on their heads, and the water of the harbour rippling below their feet, and smiled at each other with pleasure. To Maggie, the sight of Nicholas Grant's square goodhumoured face seemed like a temporary reprieve from Blake's anger. She liked Nicholas and had enjoyed his undemanding company on the one or two dates they had had. He was always easy and kind and thoughtful, and she could never understand how his wife could bear to leave him. 'I'm afraid she didn't find me very exciting, that's all there was to it,' was the dry explanation he offered, and he never spoke of her to Maggie again, but she had seen the pain behind his crooked smile, and had understood only too well the agony of loving someone who didn't love you.

His eyes were creased at the corners as he leaned forward and kissed her now. 'A privilege to kiss the bride,' he smiled. 'I missed the chance at your wedding. Tell me, how did everything go off?'

'Oh, very well indeed. We had a lovely day for it.' Maggie returned his smile brilliantly.

'Good, I'm glad. You deserve to be happy, Maggie, if ever a girl deserves it. Blake's a lucky fellow, I hope he knows it.'

It was a conventionally light remark, but it hit Maggie where it hurt most and she winced involuntarily.

Nicholas leaned towards her, frowning. 'Are you O.K., Maggie? You look all in.'

She swallowed, fighting a desire to howl, just because Nicholas had noticed the way she was looking and feeling. Blake certainly hadn't, or if he had he wasn't showing any sympathy.

She grinned wryly. 'I seem to be a rotten traveller, that's all it is. It's been a long flight and the journey isn't over yet.'

He looked down at the luggage at her feet. 'Where are you off to now?'

'We're going to Macao. Blake's taking me there for the weekend.'

'Bright idea,' approved Nicholas. 'Just the place for a honeymoon—a romantic spot, and quiet. The very opposite of Hong Kong.'

A quiet romantic spot! And Blake would have her alone there, to punish her as he wanted! She felt suddenly dizzy and swayed on her feet. Nicholas's arm shot out to steady her and he clicked his tongue worriedly. 'He's not going to have a honeymoon at all if he doesn't take better care of his wife. Where's he got to, by the way? Ah, here he is.'

Blake came striding towards them. 'Nick Grant! What the hell are you doing here? I thought you were in Mexico.'

The eyes of the two men met and suddenly there was a kind of tension between them that Maggie had never noticed before.

'I was, and now I'm here,' Nicholas said shortly. 'But we won't go into that now, there are more important things to be attended to. Your new wife seems in need of care and attention.' He spoke lightly, but the set of his mouth denoted a certain criticism.

Blake looked down at Maggie, still enclosed by Nicholas's supporting arm, and his face hardened fleetingly. 'Weddings are apt to be something of a strain, aren't they—darling?' He gave her what she recognised as a falsely loving smile and grasped her arm, pulling her out of Nicholas's grasp. 'She'll be fine when we get to Macao. She can't wait, can you, my love?' His fingers dug into the soft flesh of her arm. 'Come along, sweetie, or the jetfoil will sail without us.' He released her arm and picked up their two travel bags. 'Thanks for your solicitude, Nick,' he said with a cool glance at the other man.

'Shall I give you a hand with your luggage?' Nicholas

offered, looking doubtfully at Maggie, as if she needed carrying too.

'No, thanks,' Blake said shortly. 'Come along—darling.' Over his shoulder he said casually to Nicholas, 'Shall I see you again before you leave?'

'I'm not leaving.' Nicholas's feet were planted firmly on the quay as if he were ready to resist any attempt to move him. 'Dave James is having family trouble, so I'm here to stand in for him and see the new project under way.'

Blake didn't look pleased. 'I see, I hadn't heard. Oh well, then, we'll contact each other in the office on Monday.'

Maggie smiled warmly at Nicholas. 'Lovely to see you, Nick, we'll meet again soon.' Reluctantly, she turned and followed Blake's tall, unyielding back.

Meeting Nicholas had worked like a shot in the arm for Maggie and knowing he would be here in Hong Kong was reassuring. He was the kind of friend one could always turn to in trouble, and she was fairly sure she was going to be in trouble soon. But meanwhile she must act as naturally as possible and hope that Blake's anger would abate and that he would become more reasonable so that they could discuss the situation.

On the upper deck of the jetfoil she looked out of the window and tried to take in the amazing scene in the harbour. She had never before travelled on such a modern, exotic craft, and she marvelled at the speed at which it skimmed and bumped over the choppy blue water. It seemed a miracle that it managed to avoid the amazing variety of vessels in the harbour. Maggie recognised the Chinese junks and sampans from photographs and films, but there were larger steamers, ferries, tankers, yachts, tiny busy motorboats, and on the far side, an enormous white ocean-going liner was pulling away from its berth.

It seemed that anything that could float on water was congregated in the vast harbour, moving at different speeds in every direction at once. It looked to Maggie extremely dangerous, but she supposed they knew what they were doing. A week ago she would have laughed about it with Blake, but now Blake was miles away from her, a remote figure behind his high wall of anger and frustration.

When they stepped off the jetfoil on to the landing stage the air was hotter and more humid than ever. Maggie longed for a breath of real sea air, the kind you get in Cornwall, or even Brighton, but the air from the sea here was just as hot as the air on the land.

She pushed back her damp brown curls and murmured, 'I think I shall end up as a little puddle on the ground fairly soon.'

It was a brave attempt at lightening the atmosphere between them, but Blake merely looked stonily down at her and said, 'You're not going to collapse on me, are you? I'm not likely to be taken in twice, you know.'

He bundled her into a taxi and she sat huddled in a corner, longing to be back in her cool bedroom at home and wishing with all her heart that she had never gone to work for Blake, never fallen in love with him.

The hotel they arrived at seemed huge and luxurious in a showy kind of way, but Maggie didn't notice much as a grinning Chinese boy took them up in a lift and deposited their luggage on the floor in an enormous bedroom.

'Everything O.K.? Thank you, sir.' The grin widened as he pocketed the tip Blake gave him and closed the door behind him.

Blake waved a hand round the room. 'Here you are, then. The bridal chamber. That was what you wanted, wasn't it?' His lip curled.

He tossed his briefcase down on a table in the window and prowled round the room, sliding back doors. 'Shower in here. I'll occupy it first while you're unpacking our cases—like a good little wife,' he added mockingly.

He stripped off his shirt and disappeared through a door on the far side of the room. A moment later the sound of splashing could be heard.

Maggie sank on to the huge bed and looked at their luggage. The room was blessedly air-conditioned and she was beginning to revive a little, but even so she didn't feel equal to the effort of struggling with the heavy cases. She lay back on the bed and closed her eyes, refusing to allow herself to imagine what was going to happen next.

A few minutes later Blake emerged, a dark green towel knotted round his middle, drops of water gleaming on his dark hair, the muscles of his arms rippling. He looked magnificent, dynamic, crackling with vitality, and Maggie's heart suddenly started to beat unevenly. If only this had been a real honeymoon, he would have come across the room and taken her in his arms and kissed her and——

She sat up. 'Have you finished with the shower? I shan't be even part-human until I've had one myself.'

He scowled at her. 'I thought I told you to unpack our cases.'

She didn't like the tone of his voice at all. Oh God, she thought, there's going to be a fight, and she didn't feel capable of fighting anyone just now, least of all this big, powerful man who stood close to the bed, glowering down at her.

She slid her legs sideways to the floor. 'I'll have a shower first,' she said, trying to make her voice ordinary, but it came out squeaky and two tones higher than usual.

He came closer. 'You'll do as I say,' he told her savagely. 'You chose to marry me, and I'll be calling the tune from now on.'

His expression changed, his eyes narrowed and he moved a little away and leaned against the door of the closet, surveying her insolently. 'And while we're on the subject,' he said, 'I may as well inspect the goods I've acquired. Wives should know the proper way to undress before their husbands. Let's see what you can do.'

She stared at him in blank horror. This was worse than she had imagined in her darkest moments, this—this travesty of lovemaking that he was demanding of her.

'No!' she gasped, her eyes wide as she pulled the limp collar of her thin suit closer round her neck. 'I can't—you can't make me——' She was shivering violently now.

He smiled nastily. 'Oh, indeed I can. I can make you do anything I choose. Go on, take off that suit—it looks a wreck anyway.'

Maggie panicked. She was on her feet in a second and stumbling towards the door, not knowing what she would do when she got through it. She only knew she must get away from the ruthless, cynical gaze in the hard grey-green eyes fixed on her with such contempt.

It was hopeless from the start. He reached her in two strides and caught her round the waist in a steely grip. 'Oh no, you don't,' he hissed. 'You made a fool of me in the church. You're not going to make a fool of me again by causing a commotion here.'

He was forcing her back towards the bed and she took refuge in quick, breathless argument. 'Blake—I *didn't* make a fool of you in the church. Don't you see, you'd have looked pretty silly if I *hadn't* turned up.'

'Don't give me that as an excuse,' he snarled. 'Are you trying to tell me you changed your mind in order to preserve my dignity? If you expect me to believe that you'll expect anything!'

He stood over her, large and formidable. 'Go on, take those clothes off. Or would you like me to do it for you?'

She cowered back as he raised his hands. 'No,' she whispered. 'I'll do it myself.'

He moved back a couple of paces. 'Go on, then.'

Maggie fumbled with the fastening of her short coat. It's nothing, she told herself desperately. You've undressed on the beach lots of times without bothering too much about how far you could keep yourself covered up. No doubt some of the men in the party have had more than a glimpse of you and you never gave it a thought. Nobody thinks anything about it these days of topless bars and nude theatre shows.

But this was different. Incredible as it might seem, this was Blake standing watching her with a taunting look on his face—*Blake*, whom she thought she had known so well, and whom she had never known at all.

Her cheeks flaming crimson, she peeled off the damp, creased jacket and threw it on the bed.

Blake's eyes never left her for a second. 'Go on,' he jeered, 'you're doing fine.'

She unfastened her skirt and let it slide to the carpet, stepping over it.

'*Now* will you let me go and take a shower?' She met his eyes in pleading.

He smiled mockingly. 'Oh, not yet.' His eyes passed over her meaningfully. 'Surely the best is still to come?'

Anything, she thought desperately, *anything* to get away from that insulting gaze! In a kind of frenzy she dragged off the final flimsy garments and stood before him naked, her cheeks flaming with misery and humiliation.

Blake stood there, his eyes passing over her slowly, insolently, from head to foot and back again. Then a small, sardonic smile touched his mouth. 'I don't remember how much the marriage licence cost me,' he sneered. 'But however much it was I doubt if the goods are worth the money.'

He turned away from her and snapped open his travel-bag. 'You can have your shower now,' he said indifferently, pulling out a silky brown shirt. 'I'll go down and order a meal and we can appear in the restaurant like a happy honeymoon couple. That'll be a good joke, won't it?' He pulled the shirt over his head, picked up a hairbrush and turned to the dressing table mirror, ignoring her.

The scalding tears threatened to choke her as she groped her way blindly towards the shower room. Inside, she closed the door and leaned against it, sobbing, allowing all her hurt and shame to pour out with her tears. Dimly she heard Blake moving about in the bedroom and then the door closing behind him.

The tears went on and on until she was gasping for breath, but they stopped at last. Shivering and utterly exhausted, she turned on the shower and stepped into the stream of tepid water.

The feeling of the cool jets of water beating against her body seemed to revive her, to start her brain working again. Maggie was no adolescent girl to wallow in emotional trauma. She had spent her years in the tough environment of the university, competing with the men on her course, and come through. She had won herself a good job and risen nearly to the top of it. She drew in a long breath and made a decision: somehow she must go on and not allow herself to be crushed and defeated by the situation. She admitted now that she had made a terrible mistake in marrying Blake against his will. She should have fallen in with his plans and let him make a mess of his life in his own way.

But she had had this stupid, romantic idea that somehow, if they were married, he might fall in love with her. And the pathetic thing was that in spite of the way he had treated her, in spite of his humiliating rejection, that hope refused to be quenched entirely.

There was still the work to share. He had pleaded with her to come out to Hong Kong with him, he valued her help that much. And surely, if they were working together they could regain their old comradeship, that would be something to work on.

And—most important of all—even if he refused to accept her as a real wife at present, they *were* still married.

She stepped out of the refreshing shower, towelled herself dry and padded back into the bedroom. The important thing was that Blake should not find her a damp, weepy mess when he came back, as he would probably expect.

She put on fresh, fragrant undies and one of the dresses she and her mother had chosen on their shopping trips—a silky little number in a beige and white pattern with a close-fitting top and slim shoulder-straps. It was clipped at the waist and swung loosely round her knees. She brushed her damp curls into a casual style, to dry as they liked, and put on a light make-up, paying particular attention to her eyes, which still showed faint traces of tears.

She surveyed herself in the mirror, smoothing a hand over her pretty breasts and allowing herself to admire her long, smooth legs. There was nothing wrong with her shape, she assured herself. Blake might reject her, but there were plenty of other men who wouldn't.

She was Maggie Webster—no, Maggie Morden—and *that* felt very strange indeed—aged twenty-four, good to look at (reasonably), lively and cheerful (usually), with an eye for the ridiculous which she had shared with Blake (until now), efficient and confident at her job (no doubt about that). What had happened had been an unfortunate mistake, but it wasn't the end of the story yet, and in spite of herself she could still feel hope.

In short, Maggie treated herself to a concentrated dose of positive suggestion, so that when Blake opened the bedroom door some time later she was able to turn and smile at him in an easy, natural way.

'Hullo,' she said. 'Have you fixed up a meal for us? I'm feeling distinctly peckish, aren't you? Shall we go down?'

She twirled before the long mirror, arms wide. 'Do I look all right? Do you like me better with clothes on?' Her brown eyes glinted with mischief.

For once Blake had no ready reply. He stared at her blankly and she saw that she had managed to surprise him. It gave her a small feeling of elation. The elation might not last—indeed she was fairly sure it wouldn't— but perhaps it would see her through the evening ahead.

'I've booked a table,' Blake announced, and seemed to have nothing to add.

'Oh, that's splendid—let's go.' Maggie linked her arm

with his as they went out to the lift.

Blake swung the lift doors shut on them and regarded her darkly. 'I'm not sure what game you're playing,' he said sourly, 'but I hope it's amusing you.'

'Oh, it is,' she told him. 'Let's play it together while we have dinner. Let's pretend all this didn't happen and we're merely here to work together.'

Waiting for his reply, she held her breath as the lift sucked them downwards. It seemed to be taking her stomach with it twice as fast as it took the rest of her.

But Blake said nothing. He led the way along carpeted passages to an enormous restaurant, crowded with diners. The sea of tables blurred before Maggie's eyes, the buzz and chatter of conversation and laughter assaulted her ears, the smell of well-cooked food made her feel slightly ill, but she held on to her resolution and kept her head high as they were led to a corner table by a smiling Chinese waiter, and handed huge menu cards.

Maggie held hers up, hiding her face from Blake. She had made her gesture and he appeared to have rejected it. If he wouldn't even speak civilly to her she really didn't know how she was going to get through the meal.

He put down his own menu card. 'What do you fancy?' he said, not looking at her. 'I believe the food is an interesting blend of Chinese and Portuguese.'

His voice was not friendly, but it was no longer hostile. Maggie could have swooned with relief. Perhaps he was ready to accept the flag of truce she had offered.

She grinned wryly. 'I'm ashamed to admit that I skipped my Chinese and Portuguese lessons at school. Will you order for me, please?'

He gave her an enigmatic look. 'Will you trust me that far?'

It was a sort of apology and her heart leapt in response. 'Of course,' she said sturdily. 'We're friends, aren't we? Back on our old terms?'

Friends—she must hang on to that. She had always known that Blake had a quick temper and that he could be very nasty indeed when he was roused. It was something that was tacitly accepted between them, a part of their good, tolerant working partnership. Usually they laughed together about it afterwards, taking it for granted just as they took for granted the fact of Maggie's habit of writing notes on scraps of paper, which Blake found irritating, although she never seemed to lose anything that mattered.

The Chinese waiter appeared beside them and Blake had a conference with him. Maggie didn't pay much attention; she couldn't have cared less what she ate. She felt a little lightheaded as she sipped the cool, spicy aperitif that was put before her. Blake had seemed more reasonable, more like his old self. Maggie had always been an optimist and it only took that to send her hopes soaring. Perhaps he would let her explain; they could talk things over and she would tell him it was because of her family, because of his career. The only thing she wouldn't tell him was that she had married him because she was crazy about him.

Above all, she must try to keep the situation from becoming too emotional again, and then—then there might be hope. Just so long as she was his wife there might be hope, she told herself once more, hanging on desperately to that single fact.

She stole a glance at him as he talked to the waiter, at his handsome saturnine face, at the way his glossy dark hair grew round his temples, at his mouth. She looked at his lips, sculptured and mobile, and her pulses began to throb heavily. Blake had never kissed her, not a man-to-woman kiss. Merely a friendly salute now and then, and that hard, cold kiss in the church vestry. But perhaps tonight, when they went to their room—Her pulses began to throb. He couldn't have meant his insulting words, spoken in anger. She had heard that for a man almost any pretty girl would do. She loved him and she would take him on any terms at all.

Their food was brought to the table and arranged skilfully in small dishes. Blake said, 'I ordered Chinese, I thought we'd be safe with that. It looks O.K.' He glanced round the crowded restaurant and added, 'This seems a popular spot, so presumably the customers are satisfied. I was given to understand that Macau was a quiet backwater of a place, but not so, evidently.' His mouth twisted sardonically. 'It's just as well we didn't yearn to leave the world behind on a honeymoon-for-two, isn't it?'

Maggie raised her neat eyebrows. 'How do you know I didn't?'

Blake frowned. 'Didn't what?'

She smiled innocently. 'Didn't want to leave the world behind on our honeymoon, of course.'

His frown deepened. 'You're in a very strange mood tonight, Maggie. I thought you suggested that we should pretend we're simply here to work together.'

'Oh dear, yes, of course I did—how silly of me.' She chuckled. 'The mention of honeymoons must have put ideas into my head.' She looked round the huge room with its decorated pillars, its highly-coloured murals, predominantly cherry-red and lemon-yellow, its glittering chandeliers, breaking up the light into millions of sparkling diamond fragments. 'It doesn't seem an awfully good spot to have a business meeting, but we'll try, if you like. How about the report for our Chinese colleagues? And when do we meet them—is it arranged yet? And——'

She was suddenly aware that someone was standing behind her chair, and turned to see Nicholas Grant.

She gave a little gasp of surprise and pleasure. 'Nick! You didn't tell us you were coming here too. Were you on the jetfoil with us?'

He walked round the table. 'I was, but you don't need three on a honeymoon. I was the soul of tact and kept out of your way until——'

'—until I ran into him in the bar just now,' Blake put in. 'When I used the occasion to make a request to him. Good old Nick,' he added with a touch of malice. 'Always ready to oblige a friend!'

Maggie stared from one man to the other. 'What are you two talking about?'

'Haven't you told her?' Nick looked vastly uncomfortable.

'Not yet, I thought we'd better enjoy our dinner first,' Blake said.

Nick nodded. 'O.K. Fair enough. Well——' he shifted from one foot to the other '—I'll join my party.' He nodded to a table in the centre of the restaurant where three men were sitting, two Chinese and one European. 'I found a few buddies here from my last visit,' he explained. 'Be seeing you,' he said. He hesitated for a moment longer and then turned away.

Maggie looked at Blake questioningly. 'What on earth was all that about?'

He fingered his wine glass, his face expressionless. 'You get on well with Nick Grant, I think? He's an old friend of yours?'

'Well, yes, I suppose so. I like Nick very much.'

'That's all right, then, because I'm leaving him to look

after you for a few days. I'm flying back to the U.K. tomorrow. I spun Nick a tale about a message that was waiting for me here and said that I have to go back to consult with my father urgently about some snag that's turned up and can't be sorted out by phone.'

'B-but that wasn't true,' she stammered. 'You haven't had any message, have you?'

'No,' he said.

'Then—then why?' Something in his face frightened her.

'I'm going back to see Fiona,' he said. 'And also to see my solicitor. I shall get him to start proceedings immediately for an annulment of this intolerable marriage.'

CHAPTER FIVE

'I JUST don't get it,' grumbled Nicholas Grant. 'I don't get it at all.' He ran his fingers through his thinning fair hair, scowling. 'The damned fellow's just married the prettiest, most delightful girl around, and he spends the first night of his honeymoon gambling in the Casino! I know he did, because I was there myself until five this morning. And I'm feeling the effects just now.' He sketched imaginary dark circles under his eyes. 'I wasn't cut out to stay up gambling all night. But I was lurked into it by my pals.'

Nick and Maggie had got right away from the gaudy hotel that looked rather like a huge ornamented tea-caddy from the outside. Blake had left on the first jetfoil with hardly another word to Maggie; he had merely come to their room, collected his luggage, said, 'I'll see you when I get back,' and departed.

Nick had been waiting for Maggie when she came down to the hotel lobby, wan and pale after a sleepless night, but smiling resolutely. Neither had felt like breakfast and they had had coffee and rolls, and now they were walking along narrow cobbled streets between overhanging houses, their balconies draped with flowers and trailing greenery.

'This is rather like Spain, isn't it?' said Maggie, hoping that Nick wasn't expecting a reply. 'I had a holiday once in——'

'Come on, love,' Nick broke in, 'don't evade the issue. You know I'm not given to prying or interfering—or I hope you do—but Blake's taken himself off and left me responsible for you, and I think I ought to know at least part of the score.' He kept his eyes straight ahead as he added, 'And seeing that Blake Morden stepped in and pinched the girl I'd picked out for myself I think I'm owed that.'

Maggie came to a sudden halt, tilting her curly brown head. 'Nick—you're joking, aren't you?'

He smiled down at her wryly. 'Never more serious. I suppose I wasn't quick enough off the mark, that's the story of my life.'

They turned out of the narrow street and came upon a small wooded park, rioting with tropical flowers whose names Maggie didn't know: huge trailing blossoms in swathes and ropes of crimson and gold and blue. A heavy scent filled the air beneath the trees.

They sat down on a carved wooden seat that looked as if it had stood there for centuries. Maggie laced her fingers together. 'Nick, I—I don't know what to say.'

'No need to say anything, my dear. I'm not trying to play the lovelorn rejected suitor.' He looked away through the trees to where an ornate Portuguese building gleamed white and pink through the leaves, like sugar icing on a cake. 'I think,' he said slowly, 'that maybe you've guessed that I'm still in love with Dora, in spite of everything that's happened, but—well, I suppose I have to admit that it's over for good, and I don't want to live alone for the rest of my life.' He turned to her and his look was gentle. 'I think you're a grand girl, Maggie, and we seemed to get on well, so—I began to think of a future we might share.'

He shrugged. 'That's the whole story, but you mustn't let it embarrass you or spoil our friendship. I'm very, very fond of you, and I want to see things go well for you. That's my excuse for butting in, so—forgive me?'

He spoke with such simplicity and sincerity that Maggie suddenly gulped. How easy life would be if everyone could talk to each other like that. She couldn't imagine Blake doing it. Blake would put up a high wall of pride and anger and you had to guess what he was thinking.

She touched Nick's arm. It felt solid and reliable beneath his thin shirt. 'Thank you for telling me, Nick, and if things had gone differently—well—who knows?'

'But you fell in love with Blake Morden?' he said quietly, and she nodded.

'A long, long time ago. I didn't think I stood a chance with him, but then—suddenly——' She stopped. That was as far as confidences could go. She said wryly, 'About your question—all I can say is we had a—a slight difference of opinion last evening.'

Nick lifted a sceptical eyebrow. '*Slight?*'

'The mother and father of a bust-up,' Maggie

admitted. She improvised quickly. 'I didn't want him to go back to England, you see.'

'I should jolly well think you didn't! He——'

'But you know Blake,' Maggie went on firmly. 'His work means a terrific lot to him and as his wife I accept that. I've got to, haven't I?' She grimaced. 'It's rather like marrying an artist or a musician. You never quite come first.'

If only it were as simple as that, she thought unhappily. But Nick seemed to accept her explanation.

He said, 'Well, I still think his new wife should have come first, but no doubt I'll hear in due course what the great work crisis was, and until then——' he looked down at her, smiling, '—I'll reserve judgment.'

'Thank you, Nick, you're a real friend,' said Maggie.

He got to his feet and took her hand to help her up, drawing it into the crook of his arm.

'Then as a friend, may I be permitted to show you round Macao? I'm not expected back at the office in Hong Kong until Monday, and I don't suppose you're expected there at all just now, so we have the rest of today and tomorrow here.'

'Thank you, that would be lovely,' Maggie said. She would make it enjoyable for Nick; she wouldn't mope and if she felt dreary she would do her best to keep it to herself.

He patted her arm as they started to walk again and said quietly, 'I'm sorry you'll be seeing Macao with the wrong man, but perhaps we can pass the time pleasantly enough.'

In a spurt of gratitude Maggie said, a little incoherently, 'You're not the wrong man, Nick, only a different man.'

Very different, she thought, with a sudden piercing

need to see Blake, to see his tall, arrogant form and the
way his grey-green eyes would meet hers with the faintest
of twinkles, acknowledging a secretly shared joke. But
that wouldn't happen again, she knew with a terrible
pang of anguish; she had forfeited the right to share a
joke with Blake. Or to share anything else. He had gone
home to start annulment proceedings and she would be
his wife for a very short time—and that in name only. It
seemed as if a long, dark tunnel were ahead of her—but
she refused to let herself stare into it.

She gave Nick's arm a little squeeze. 'Let's go, then,'
she said. 'Where do we start?'

'At the tourist office, I suggest. They'll be able to give
us all the gen, so we won't miss anything.'

That was the beginning of Maggie's two days in
Macao. Two days when she hovered on the brink of
tears so often that she had to turn her head away quickly
from Nick so that he shouldn't see how she was feeling.
He was such a delightful companion, so kind and con-
siderate, that she felt guilty because she couldn't manage
to enjoy anything. It was a long weary charade when
she had to be on her guard all the time.

After something of a search they found the tourist
office, tucked away in a back room of an old house on
the waterfront. Here they obtained maps and a guide-
book.

'What a fabulous house!' Maggie exclaimed as they
made their way back through graceful, high-ceilinged
reception rooms, full of heavy carved furniture, with
doors opening out into intimate little courtyards, where
tropical flowers tumbled about in profusion and mosses
crept through the cracks in the crumbling stones of the
walls. 'It all seems so old and full of history.'

'It probably is,' Nick told her. 'Macau has a distinctly

racy and somewhat disreputable past. I'll tell you what I know about it when we've seen the sights.'

In the end they decided that it was much too hot for any serious sightseeing. They wandered in a leisurely way through the quiet old cobbled streets with their faded façades of Portuguese buildings, some of them colour-washed in pink and lime and pale yellow which, Nick told her, were the typical Portuguese architectural colours. They sat under the trees outside a café on the *avenida* and drank lemon tea, and Nick recounted what he had learned about the history of Macao, when it served as an international port for trade between China and Europe.

'Until Britain blotted her copybook in the last century,' he added, with a grin, 'by shipping huge quantities of opium from India and Turkey into China, through Macao. Naturally, the Chinese objected. They didn't want all their workers living in a perpetual opium-haze. Eventually a war was fought over it—two wars, in fact. France joined in the second one. It's a long story, but in the end the West won, and Macao stayed a Portuguese province. That was more or less when Britain gained a long lease on Hong Kong, too.'

'It's fascinating,' said Maggie. For a few minutes she had managed to lose herself in the story that Nick was telling, and to put the thought of Blake out of her mind. But inevitably it came back, like a solid lump inside her that wouldn't move. He had gone and he had taken her life with him, and it was just a ghost that was walking about Macao with Nick, smiling and laughing and listening to his stories.

That first day she dined with Nick at the hotel and went off to bed early, on his advice. 'You say you don't get jet-lag, but all the same you must be tired. Have a good night's sleep, and tomorrow evening we'll be wicked and go to the Casino.'

To her surprise, Maggie slept heavily and wakened with the determination to fill every moment of the day, to crowd out of her mind her longing for Blake.

'Let's see all there is to see,' she suggested to Nick at breakfast in the hotel.

From the start the day was a disappointment. It was even hotter than the previous day and their thin shirts were soaked through in minutes. But at Maggie's insistence they carried on. If she could get utterly exhausted perhaps she could throw off her misery, before it overcame her and she made a fool of herself in front of Nick—which was the very last thing she wanted to do.

Eventually, tired and hot, they came out in front of the vast, empty, vaguely menacing façade of the seventeenth-century church of Sao Paulo and found from their guide book that it was built by fugitive Japanese Christians from Nagasaki and nearly destroyed by a typhoon in the nineteenth century. The architect in Nick was fascinated and he spent the best part of an hour poking about what remained of the great building, while Maggie got hotter and hotter and more and more exhausted until, noticing her plight, he was suddenly overcome by contrition and found a taxi to take them back to the hotel.

In the afternoon, after a shower and a siesta, they visited the Protestant Cemetery, which, the guide book told them, was a historical document in itself. They found the final resting-place of one of Winston Churchill's ancestors, and of the first Protestant missionary to China. But when they came upon the graves of the young midshipmen, some of them only seventeen or eighteen years old, who had died in Macao Roads,

or of fever in the Opium Wars, it was all too much for
Maggie. She was moved unbearably, and the tears that
she shed for the unfortunate boys mingled with the tears
for her own unhappiness.

Nick was worried by her distress. 'We shouldn't have
come here,' he said, holding her while she sobbed on his
shoulder.

Maggie lifted her head away at last, blew her nose
and grinned shakily. 'Stupid of me,' she quavered. 'I'm
not usually a weepy type. It must be the heat, I think.'
She glanced around at the other people in the cemetery—two or three small parties who looked like tourists. One of the women seemed to be looking curiously
at her. 'Come on, let's go, shall we?' she said to Nick.
'I'm just an embarrassment to you at the moment.'

'Rubbish!' he said stoutly, but she thought his face
was a shade redder than it had been before, and guessed
he was the kind of man who would avoid anything in
the nature of a public spectacle.

He put his arm firmly around her. 'We'll go back to
the hotel and you shall have a good long rest before
dinner.' He looked down on her curly brown head, bent
low as she stumbled beside him over the baked ground.
'You're missing that husband of yours, too, aren't you,
Maggie?' he said so kindly that she began to cry again.

'Is it always as hot as this?' Maggie gasped, as they left
the cemetery.

Nick mopped his brow with a damp handkerchief.
'At this time of the year, yes. We're just about in the
tropics here and it's typhoon time.'

'Oh, gosh!' Maggie grinned weakly. 'I hadn't reckoned
on typhoons. Are they bad ones?' It only needed a typhoon,
she thought, to add to all the other storms.

'All kinds, but the bad ones only turn up now and again. Still, it's not, I'd say, the best time of the year to choose for a honeymoon,' he added wryly.

'There wasn't any choice. Once we'd decided to get married it had to be now, because of the work starting in Hong Kong.' She summoned a laugh to show that she wasn't criticising Blake. 'But I didn't mind. I'm keen on the work too, you know. I'm used to being Blake's assistant, and that won't change, I'm still going to work with him.'

But was she? As they made their way back to the hotel she asked herself that question and the answer came back like a sharp blade through her heart: Yes, of course it would change. Once the marriage was dissolved Blake wouldn't have her with him at any price. He hated her for what she had done, he'd shown that very clearly.

Nick was saying that Blake was a lucky man to have found a wife who was a help to him in his work and was interested in it. 'It must make all the difference,' he added sadly, and Maggie knew he was thinking of his own broken marriage.

'Nick, I——' She had a sudden impulse to confide in him, to tell him the whole story, to enlist his understanding, and perhaps sympathy.

'Yes?' She heard a certain eagerness in his voice. Perhaps he sensed that she was about to tell him something that would draw them closer together, would turn a friendship into something deeper. Could he possibly have guessed that things were going very wrong between herself and Blake?

She resisted the temptation. It would raise too many questions that she wasn't prepared to look in the face yet.

'I'll be glad to get back to the hotel and have a shower,' she finished lamely.

He looked rather hard at her for a moment. Then he said, in his easy way, 'Me too,' and they walked on.

As Nick had suggested, he took Maggie to the Casino that night. 'You don't need to play if you don't want to,' he promised her, 'but you can't leave Macao without seeing the one thing that keeps the place alive now—gambling.'

'Is it very daring—what do I wear?' Maggie asked, with visions of beautiful spies in exotic gowns and elegant men in immaculate dinner jackets.

Nick assured her that it didn't matter in the least, adding a little shyly that whatever she wore she would look delightful. 'But it's not a bit like Monte Carlo or Deauville. Not really black-tie-and-cabin-cruiser-out-in-the-bay.'

He was right, she discovered, as they made their way through the hotel to the vast suite of gaming rooms. All the tables were packed with people playing and watching, and it looked more like a day at the races than what Maggie had imagined a casino would look like. Certainly her own casual dress of pale blue embroidered cotton was very much in the style of the rest of the company there. Some of the women wore quite elaborate cheongsams in gorgeous colours, but the tourists were dressed quite casually and the men certainly hadn't dressed formally. There seemed to be many different kinds of game in progress on the green-baize-covered tables under the brilliant low-shaded lights, and Nick started to explain them to Maggie, but it made her head spin.

She stared round the crowded, buzzing, smoke-hazed room with its archways into other crowded rooms.

'Where on earth do all the people come from?' she asked Nick.

'Hong Kong mostly. There's a no-gambling law in Hong Kong, so they have to come over here at weekends for a flutter. A good many Japanese tourists patronise the place too, parties of 'em. Look at that lot over there. They seem to be enjoying themselves anyway.'

Everybody, it seems, was having a good time, and Maggie tried to enter into the spirit of the place. Nick bought her some counters and showed her how to place them. She found herself fascinated by the tension and the excitement when the wheel spun and the croupier's long rake pushed and pulled at the little heaps of coloured counters on the board, and after half an hour she found to her amazement that she had three times as many counters as she had started with.

'Lucky girl!' Nick laughed as she piled up her counters. But Maggie was remembering something her grandmother used to say when the family gathered to play card games on a Saturday evening. 'Lucky at cards, unlucky in love,' Gran had intoned solemnly from her chair by the fire. Gran had been gone for years and years, so why did she have to remember that now?

'I don't think I want to play any more,' she said, getting up quickly, and in spite of Nick's insistence she firmly refused to accept her winnings when he had exchanged the counters. 'Keep them and put them in the next charity box you see,' she said. 'I'm no gambler.'

She felt that somehow her refusal to accept the money might make the old prediction untrue.

It was as they were leaving the Casino that Nick was hailed from across the hall. Maggie looked round to see a tall man with crisply waving fair hair, and recognised the European member of the party that Nick had been with in the dining room two nights ago. He had a Chinese girl on his arm tonight, and Maggie had a swift impression of an exquisite work of art. Everything about her was perfection: the jade-green cheongsam cleverly draped, showed off the delicate curves of the lovely young figure. The glossy black hair was arranged in wings that caressed the creamy skin of the oval face. Jade rings hung from the tiny ears and the tilted black eyes were alight with fun.

'Dietrich! Well met again!' Nick clapped the tall man on the shoulder. 'I thought you were going back this morning.'

'We were, but Ling San thought she'd like another day here.'

The Chinese girl laughed, a pretty tinkling sound. 'Dietrich left me alone two nights to go gambling,' she grumbled. 'I thought I should gamble a bit too.' She spoke perfect English with a faint American accent.

'Well done, Ling San.' Nick turned to Maggie. 'Maggie, meet Dietrich Hauser, a very good friend of mine, and his wife Ling San.' He took Maggie's hand, drawing her forward. 'This is another good friend of mine—Maggie Morden. I'm looking after her while her husband is away in the U.K.'

'Lucky Nick!' smiled Ling San mischievously, while they were all shaking hands.

As is the way with such encounters, it was decided to repair to one of the hotel bars for a drink and a gossip. Maggie soon discovered that Dietrich Hauser was the Hong Kong representative of a German banking company, and that he and Ling San had been married only a few months.

'And how long have you been married, Maggie?' Ling San enquired.

Maggie felt her cheeks flush as she replied, 'Nearly a week.'

There was a short silence and she could almost hear what the two opposite were thinking. Only a week and he's gone back to the U.K. without her!

'You haven't met her husband, Blake Morden, have you, Dietrich?' Nick put in rather too hastily.

The German shook his blond head, his bright blue eyes fixed on Maggie thoughtfully. 'Not yet. The word has gone round that he's coming to H.K. to put up the new Elizabeth Complex out at Shatin.'

'Not at Shatin,' Maggie put in quickly. 'That was the original idea, but the site has been changed since then.'

Nick smiled at her and then at the other two. 'Maggie will be working on the job with Blake, when he returns,' he said. 'She's an expert in her own right, I may tell you.'

Ling San exclaimed, 'You are a builder? I think that is wonderful! I like to hear of women doing important things. I, too, may do important things one day.'

She laughed up at her handsome husband, who gazed back at her proudly. 'Ling San thinks of starting her own—what do you call it, *liebling*?—beauty shop, isn't it?' and Ling San nodded her glossy little head enthusiastically.

'What a marvellous idea,' Maggie put in. 'May I be your first customer?'

It was all very pleasant and friendly, and when they finally rose to part it had been agreed that Maggie should visit the Hausers' flat in Hong Kong when they all returned there the following day.

Dietrich and Ling San went into the gaming rooms and Maggie and Nick wandered out of the hotel on to the waterfront. It was still very hot and humid, although the sound of the gently lapping water in the darkness seemed to make the air feel cooler. 'Ling San's a darling, isn't she?' Maggie sighed. 'And so lovely! Somehow you don't think of Chinese women as being so glamorous. I suppose it's the picture we have of mainland China, with all the women in baggy trousers and those peaked caps.'

Nick laughed. 'I can't see Ling San in a peaked cap. The Hong Kong Chinese are quite different, of course, and Dietrich is extremely prosperous. He can indulge his little wife in every way. He adores her excessively.'

Maggie was silent as they stood looking over the sweep of the bay, with the myriad lights from the hotel behind throwing coloured reflections on to the smooth water. It was so peaceful under the banyan trees. The pools of shadow seemed to enclose them intimately. And the treacherous longing came back in a flood, for Blake to be there beside her. She yearned for him so painfully that she could almost believe that one could die of love.

Nick said, 'Over there is the island of——' He broke off. 'Why, what's wrong, Maggie? You're crying!'

Her shoulders were shaking as she fought to control her tears and Nick's arm came round her comfortingly. He held her close against him, as he had held her in the cemetery, and she buried her head against his shirt and sobbed her heart out. He didn't try to stop her. He thought she was missing Blake and that was all there was to it, of course.

'Poor little Maggie,' he said softly, and put his cheek against her hair. 'It's a hell of a honeymoon for you, but he'll soon be back.'

He pulled out a folded handkerchief and she mopped her eyes. 'I don't know why you put up with me, Nick, I'm really wet just now, in every way. I think you should forget about me and leave me to mope on my own.'

He was looking down at her, but she couldn't see the expression on his face. He said huskily, 'It would take more than a few tears to persuade me to do that, my dear.' And before she realised what he was going to do he had bent and kissed her.

His kiss was slow and gentle, not exactly a kiss of consolation but not an invitation to passion either. Gratefully Maggie kissed him back and whispered, 'You are a darling, Nick. I almost wish——'

He put a large hand over her mouth. 'Don't say it,' he laughed rather unevenly, 'or you'll be putting ideas into my head! Now, come along, to bed with you, my girl, and tomorrow morning we go back to Hong Kong. What with all the bustle there the time will fly, you'll see, and it won't seem any time at all until Blake's back with you.'

They made their way back to the hotel arm-in-arm, and neither of them took much notice of the little group of people they met coming out. If they had done Maggie might have recognised the red hair and curious eyes of the woman who had seemed to be so interested in them earlier in the day, in the cemetery.

Nick was right about Hong Kong. From the moment they stepped off the jetfoil on to the ferry pier Maggie was aware of the brash, exciting atmosphere of the place. A taxi took them from the ferry through streets congested with traffic to the offices that the Morden Corporation had leased on the top floor of a towering white skyscraper overlooking the harbour. The office was humming with activity already, although the actual building work wasn't due to start for a couple of weeks.

A small team had been sent out from London and

reinforced by local talent—several earnest, well-dressed young Chinese men bent industriously over their desks or drawing-tables.

'Wonderful workers, the Chinese,' Nick whispered, as they passed through the main office to the Manager's section. 'They're so anxious to make their way and get rich that it's unbelievable the amount of work they'll get through.'

One or two of the office staff from London were already vaguely known to Maggie, and she smiled at them as she walked beside Nick. She was conscious of the odd looks they gave her. No doubt the news of her marriage to Blake Morden had reached Hong Kong through the Corporation grapevine already, and it was only natural that they should be curious to see the girl who had captured the Chairman's son—the charismatic Blake Morden. If only they knew just how much satisfaction it had brought her, she thought with a pang.

In the Manager's office a tall, grizzled man with a narrow, clever face got up from his desk to greet them. Robert Denby was one of the Corporation's most trusted senior officers and although Maggie had never had much to do with him in the course of her work, she was familiar with his reputation as a stickler for discipline—a man who guarded jealously the reputation and good name of the Morden Corporation.

He came round the desk, holding out his hand to her. 'Mrs Morden—delighted to welcome you to Hong Kong.' He nodded a greeting to Nick and pulled out a chair for Maggie. 'Your husband called in to see me before he flew back to London. How unfortunate that he should be recalled when you'd only just arrived. However, he explained to me that Nicholas here was looking after your comfort, and I hope you haven't been too put out by the change of arrangements.'

Maggie sank into the chair, somewhat overcome by this rather ponderous speech and smiled politely, not being able to think of any reply.

The Manager pressed a buzzer on his desk. 'You would like coffee I'm sure, Mrs Morden. I'll get my secretary to produce one.'

The door opened to admit a rather plain, red-haired young woman whose face was vaguely familiar to Maggie. As her pale eyes alighted on Maggie she blinked quickly but gave no other sign of recognition. She turned to the Manager. 'Yes, Mr Denby?'

'Mrs Morden has just arrived from Macau, Dorothy,' he said. 'Do you think you could provide her with a coffee? And one for Mr Grant too, of course.'

The red-haired secretary's eyes went to Maggie again, then to Nick, who smiled at her.

'Hullo, Dorothy, how are you?' Nick evidently knew her. 'Enjoying Hong Kong?'

She blinked again. She had very light eyelashes, which gave her a slightly foxy look. 'Oh, I'm fine, thank you, Mr Grant,' she mumbled, and slid quickly out of the office and closed the door.

Well, thought Maggie, what's *her* mind? Then she forgot all about it as Mr Denby launched into a long account to Nick of a consignment of air-conditioning units which had apparently been lost somewhere on route from Japan. She tried to concentrate on what they were saying, in case she should be involved later on in dealing with the matter. Then she stopped listening, as she remembered that as soon as Blake got back she would be concerned no longer with the business of the Morden Corporation.

They drank their coffee and managed eventually to

get away from Mr Denby and his complaints. Nick showed Maggie his own small drawing-office and the much larger office that had been allocated to Blake and herself to share.

'It's a super office,' She walked over to the wide plate-glass window and stood looking down over the harbour far below, thronged with shipping of all descriptions. 'Super!' she repeated, and could have wept as she thought of Blake sharing it with someone else when she had gone.

Nick joined her at the window. 'Nice view,' he observed casually, looking down into her face. He added tentatively, 'You *are* looking forward to working here with Blake on this job, aren't you, Maggie?'

She almost panicked. Nick was perceptive; he was on the verge of finding out that something was really wrong.

'Oh yes, it's what I want more than anything in the world,' she told him, and that was the truth anyway.

There was a short silence, then he said, 'That's all right, then,' but she wasn't sure she had convinced him.

He took her arm. 'Come along, then, I'm going to take you to the hotel where we're all being housed for the duration.'

A taxi deposited them, with Maggie's luggage, at a large hotel a short distance out from the centre of the city. Blake, as befitted his status, had an elegant suite of rooms on the twenty-third floor.

When the porter had left them Nick said, 'You'll be comfortable here until Blake gets back?'

Maggie looked round the spacious rooms. 'The lap of luxury,' she said lightly.

Nick said, 'My room is a much humbler affair a few floors down, overlooking the car park.' He gave her the number and told her to contact him at any time if she needed assistance.

'Of course I will,' said Maggie, 'and thank you for looking after me so well, but I'm sure I can stand on my own two feet now. I mustn't impose on your good nature any longer.'

Nick gave her an odd look. 'If you think I'm going to let you cope on your own you're dead wrong, my girl. Blake left me as a stand-in for him and a stand-in I shall remain, however inadequate.' He stood quite still, looking down into her face, a half-smile on his mouth, his eyes soft. 'You'll not object, Maggie?'

Suddenly she choked up and was unable to speak. She shook her head dumbly.

'That's O.K., then.' He looked pleased. 'I'll ring you later on and we'll fix a time for dinner.' He turned and went out of the room rather quickly.

Maggie sank down on to the bed. She was almost sure now that Nick guessed that all was not well between her and Blake, and that he was going to be on the spot to step into Blake's place if he could.

She sighed deeply, wondering how things were going to turn out.

The days passed. It was nearly a week since Blake had left Macao and Maggie had heard nothing from him.

Part of each day she spent at the office, although there was little she could do without Blake's direction at this stage. But at least she could hold a watching brief and familiarise herself with the office set-up. Just as if, she thought dismally, she was going to be there to see the work through.

The office staff welcomed her as one of themselves. They were a friendly bunch—all except Mr Denby's red-haired secretary, Dorothy Steel.

'Don't take any notice of her,' advised Joan, who was in charge of the typists. 'She's always a bit of a pain in the neck. She got a thing about Nick Grant back in London, a few months ago, and she's probably feeling livid that he should be taking care of you until Mr Morden comes back.'

Nick was taking care of her very thoroughly indeed. With the work at this stage he seemed able to please himself how much time he took off.

He and Maggie lunched together each day and in the afternoons they pretended they were tourists and explored Hong Kong. In the daytime the crowded streets were colourful enough, with the shop-windows packed with tempting goods, the street markets like Aladdin's caves, stacked with every fruit and vegetable imaginable, and gaudy with the reds and yellows and blues of the banners that hung low over the heads of the teeming crowds that thronged the streets, shouting to make themselves heard as they haggled and bargained with the stallholders. Maggie couldn't understand at first why the shop signs should all hang downwards, until Nick pointed out that Chinese characters read up and down, and not from left to right.

But if Hong Kong was brash and exciting in the day-time, at night it was fantastic. One night Nick took Maggie on the Peak Tram to the highest point of Hong Kong Island and they looked down on the dazzling lights that turned Hong Kong and Kowloon, below, into a fairyland. High up on the Peak the lights shone whitely through the trees, while farther down in Central District the glow was more golden, and the great blaze of coloured neon lights was reflected far out in the water of the harbour.

They stood on the heights, looking down, and up here there was a mercifully cool breeze. Nick said suddenly, 'Have you heard anything from Blake? Telex? Phone call?'

Maggie shook her head. 'Not a word.'

'He should be coming back soon. Things are going to be held up, waiting for him if he isn't careful.'

'Yes,' said Maggie. There seemed nothing else to say. The days and nights had taken on a completely unreal quality and her life had no meaning or direction any longer.

She visited the little Chinese wife of Nick's German banker friend, and listened to Ling San's plans for her beauty shop.

'I love to change a girl's looks,' Ling San explained. 'It gives her such a kick to look quite different.' She put her little head on one side and added, 'I could make *you* look quite different, Maggie.'

Maggie smiled. 'Better?'

'Oh, I don't mean that,' the kind Ling San said hastily. 'Just different. Your hair is so pretty.' She sighed. 'I envy Western girls their hair. Ours is always so much the same, whatever we do to it. If you had yours cut and shaped—so——' she gathered the shining brown curls up in one hand, tweaking out a wisp here, a frond there. 'You see?' She led Maggie to a mirror.

Maggie stared at her reflection. She had always taken her appearance for granted. So long as she looked groomed and glowingly healthy she hadn't thought much about it. As she grew up in her teens she was aware that most of her friends had become almost obsessed with their looks. They talked about nothing but clothes, hair-styles, make-up. But somehow Maggie had missed out on all that. She had been too busy working for her A-levels and after that for her degree, and in her spare time she had preferred tennis or badminton or swimming to discos.

The local boys seemed to her very young and rather gauche, and even more so by the time she had started to work at Mordens and had caught sight of Blake Morden. Maggie never knew when she had fallen in love with Blake, but it was long before she rose to the position of his assistant.

Looking at her reflection now she wondered fleetingly if it would have made any difference if she had set herself out to charm him, as his girl-friends did, if she had pored over the beauty magazines and haunted the dress departments in the Kensington store where her mother shopped.

Would Blake have seen her less as a capable colleague, a 'good sort', and more as a desirable young woman if she had looked more glamorous? She didn't know, but it was too late now even to contemplate it.

She smiled at the pretty Chinese girl. 'Yes, I see what you mean, Ling San. Perhaps, one day, I'll let you try to make me over.'

'When I get my shop you shall be my first customer,' Ling San bubbled enthusiastically.

Just a week after Blake had left for England it was arranged that the staff should make up a party to go to Aberdeen, to dine at one of the famous floating restaurants there. Maggie tried to get out of it, but Nick persuaded her to go along. 'It'll keep up your spirits,' he'd joked. 'until Himself sees fit to return.'

She thought she heard, once again, the edge of criticism in his voice. Nick thought that Blake was treating her shabbily. 'He'll be back soon,' she said brightly, 'and then I shan't need parties to keep my spirits up.'

'Well, come along just the same,' Nick urged, and she agreed to go, rather than spend the evening alone in the hotel.

She looked through the clothes hanging in her closet and finally selected the most glamorous of the dresses she had brought—a scarlet chiffon, with glittery sequin trim on the shoulder-straps and across the low-cut top. Her mother had chosen it, she remembered. 'I've heard that Hong Kong society is very sophisticated,' she had said seriously. 'You'll want to feel right.' Maggie had thought the dress rather too flashy for her, and had never imagined she would wear it, but suddenly tonight she had a feeling that she must look confident and radiant, as a new bride should look, whatever she might be feeling inside.

The party was a success. They went by taxi to Aberdeen, to where junks and sampans were jammed so close together that you could hardly see the water of the harbour in between. Nick, who knew about Hong Kong, told her that there were more than twenty thousand people living on three thousand of these picturesque but rather ramshackle vessels in the harbour. It was a strange way of life, Maggie thought, but the people seemed happy enough, and the children skipped around from one sampan to the next like little monkeys. Lines of washing hung out everywhere and cooking smells did nothing to sweeten the humid evening air.

The party was ferried out to the enormous floating restaurant, blazing with neon lights. They dined of expensive and succulent seafood and drank the local wine, and as the evening progressed they became very merry indeed. Maggie laughed and joked with them all and Nick put his head close to hers and told her she looked fabulous.

The sour looks that Mr Denby's red-haired secretary aimed at her told her the same thing, but she didn't care. Tonight she was past caring about anything.

It was late when they arrived back at the hotel. Maggie and Nick went up in the lift together. 'We'll take the express lift to your floor,' he said, 'and I'll walk down to my room.'

Maggie never knew whether he really intended to walk down again or not. Outside the door of her suite they stopped while she fumbled for her key.

'Am I to be invited in for a drink?' Nick said quietly.

In the soft-carpeted corridor they stood looking at each other, and a strange recklessness overcame Maggie. Later on, she knew, she might be sorry, but at this moment the thought of going into an empty room, alone, was not to be borne.

'Why not?' She met his questioning eyes with a smile.

In the tiny entrance lobby Nick took the silk shawl from her bare shoulders and kept his arm there instead. She leaned closer to him. Nick was a darling—strong, dependable, uncomplicated, mature. When her marriage to Blake was over, she told herself hazily, perhaps——

Arms entwined, they walked together through the door of the sitting room.

There they stopped dead. Nick's arm dropped to his side and Maggie nearly toppled over, her eyes staring, her mouth opening with shock.

Blake got up from the sofa and walked towards them, and his face was like thunder.

'So——' he said grimly, 'it was true what I've been hearing.' He put his dark face close to Nick's and there was a dangerous light in his eyes. 'You bastard, Nick

Grant,' he ground out, 'I asked you to keep an eye on my wife, not to take advantage of my absence to get into bed with her!'

CHAPTER SIX

NICK backed away a couple of paces. His face had gone very pale. 'Now, wait a minute, Blake.'

Blake was in no mood to wait. 'Get out!' he snarled. 'Get the hell out of here before I forget you're working for my firm!'

Nick hesitated, looking uncertainly at Maggie, but she nodded.

'All right, I'll go if you say so, Maggie. And when you've succeeded in making this suspicious so-and-so see what an idiot he's making of himself, we'll all have a drink together.'

The door closed behind him and Blake turned on Maggie. Before he spoke she saw how exhausted he looked; his face was haggard and there were great sooty grooves under his grey eyes.

She put a hand on his arm. 'Blake, don't jump to conclusions. Don't say anything now—not until you've had a sleep. You're too tired to be reasonable.'

He let out a harsh laugh and shook her hand off. 'Oh no, you don't get round me like that, my girl. I want to know what's been going on between you and Nick Grant while I've been out of the way. I've come back to find out, and by God, I mean to!'

He towered over her, his eyes piercing into hers, and a bitter hostility engulfed her, like a wind straight from the polar regions. She shrank away and stumbled across the room, frightened of what he meant to do next. This was a new Blake, this icy accusing man who had once been her friend. Oh God, she thought helplessly, how did we ever get like this?

She said uncertainly, 'What do you mean—you've come back to find out?'

'Exactly what I say. I dislike very much having my wife the subject of gossip among the staff out here. It undermines my authority and makes me look a fool. I won't have it, Maggie, do you hear? I bloody well won't have it!'

She turned away hopelessly. If he had been jealous she would have welcomed his anger, but this wasn't jealousy, only a cold resentful indignation. All he cared about was his standing and reputation in the company.

She shook her head wearily. 'I don't know what you're talking about. There's been nothing between Nick and me that anyone could take exception to. You left me alone in a strange place and you asked him to look after me. He's done just that, and he's done it wonderfully.'

He looked down at her flushed face. 'I bet he has,' he jeered.

The flush deepened, but she kept her head high and looked straight into his mocking face. 'Yes, he has,' she repeated firmly. 'He's done all he could to try to make up to me for what he thought was my unhappiness at having my honeymoon cut short. I didn't tell him that it wasn't a honeymoon at all, that my husband had gone out of his way to insult and humiliate me.'

Blake lounged back against the door of the shower-room, a hateful, ironic smile on his mouth. 'Do you expect me to believe that was all there was to it?'

She shrugged. 'I don't care much what you believe, Blake. Whatever there's been between you and me in the past—friendship, understanding—is dead. You're like a stranger now, an enemy, and you obviously feel the same.' Her throat was tight as she forced out the words. 'So the sooner we part the better. I suppose you've already started proceedings for an annulment of the marriage?'

She turned away and stood with her back to him, leaning the palms of her hands on the dressing table as if she were in actual physical pain. She couldn't bear to see his face, triumphant, when he told her.

He said in a flat voice. 'There isn't going to be an annulment.'

She spun round, her brain reeling. Had he changed his mind? Was he going to accept her as his wife after all? 'Then w-what——' she stammered.

'It wasn't as easy as I'd supposed. The legal situation could be complicated.' His mouth twisted bitterly. 'It seems, my darling wife, that I'm stuck with you for the present.'

She sank down on to the dressing-table stool as her knees buckled under her. This was something she had never expected.

He came close, leaning down to her, speaking in a low rasping voice. 'So you see, perhaps, why I was concerned about what you were getting up to here, in my absence. When I heard about the gossip that was going the rounds of the staff here——'

'Wait a minute,' Maggie broke in desperately. 'What gossip? What have you heard, and who's been telling lies about Nick and me?'

'Oh, not lies, surely?' His voice had a hateful smoothness now. He threw himself down on the bed, leaning back, hands in pockets, his long legs thrust out in front of him. 'But if you must know, I happened to phone Denby from London. When we'd finished our business, he started humming and hawing like an old woman, and then he came out with it. He thought I ought to know—it was very awkward for him, but he felt it his duty as manager—his secretary had made him aware of what was going on, and she was very upset and worried too——' He mimicked Mr Denby's high-pitched, querulous voice. '*So* embarrassing, when Mr Nicholas Grant was attached to the company—did my wife realise that Hong Kong society had rather conventional standards about the way a top executive's wife should behave—it could do the Corporation's reputation considerable harm with our friends out here—perhaps I'd better put in a word of warning to my wife——'

Maggie listened, getting colder and colder until her whole body felt numb. This was Dorothy Steel's doing, of course. Maggie remembered now where she had seen the girl before, that day she and Nick went to the cemetery in Macau she had been with a party of tourists there. She must have recognised Nick, and later realised that it was she, Blake Morden's wife, who was there with him. And probably Dorothy had seen them together in the Casino gardens too.

She ran a hand distractedly through her hair. 'There was nothing—nothing——' she blurted out. But even as she said the words she knew that if Blake hadn't been here tonight those words might not have been true; that the strain of the last days might very well have thrown her into Nick's arms to seek consolation, and that she would have regretted it afterwards.

He must have heard the hint of evasion in her voice, for his mouth twisted in contempt. 'Nothing? Do you expect me to believe that? When you two were seen several times kissing and cuddling, when he came to your room at night—*my* room—God, it makes me sick to think of it! And to hear it from Denby and know he was loving every minute of it——'

He stood up and gripped her shoulders, thrusting his face down only inches from hers. 'Couldn't you have behaved yourself decently while I was away? Haven't you done me enough harm without carrying on like a low-down, common little tart?'

Her head jerked back and her eyes went wide. Somehow she flung off his hands and jumped up to confront him. 'Don't you dare call me that, Blake Morden. Don't you dare!' she blazed. Automatically her hand went up and she struck him hard across his cold, sneering face.

His expression changed. The irony disappeared and she saw rage take its place. She had a moment of desperate fear; she had gone too far.

A muscle was working in his cheek. He gripped her by both arms and shook her. 'I said tart and that's what I meant. Good God, look at you, you even look like a tart! This dress——' he tugged at the flimsy sequinned shoulder-strap of the scarlet dress and it snapped in his hand. 'See?' he snarled. 'Easy, isn't it?'

She tried to grab at the bodice, but he had ripped it down. 'If anyone is going to enjoy your favours tonight it should be your husband, don't you agree?' His hand was moving over her breasts, not gently, but his touch aroused an appalling hunger in her. She didn't care what he thought of her, how much he despised her. Self-respect meant nothing at this moment. As his hands found the slit in the skirt of her dress and started to stroke her thigh she pressed herself against him recklessly, lifting her face, her lips aching to feel his lips on them.

His dark, angry face was only inches above hers. She heard him mutter hoarsely, 'So that's it, is it, that's what you want. All right, then, you shall have it, my dear.'

His mouth covered hers in a deep, merciless kiss that bruised and ravaged the tender skin until she felt she couldn't stand the pressure. But she was past caring. She had waited so long, and if this was the only way she could have Blake—in fury, not in love—then this way it must be. Her arms went up round his neck and her fingers buried themselves deeply in the thick hair as he bent her back, his kisses savaging her mouth, her breast.

Then he lifted her roughly in his arms and tossed her on to the bed, pulling off her dress with one hand, while his other hand fumbled with the buttons of his own shirt. She felt the heat and hardness of his skin against hers and her body arched in sudden overpowering response.

Sometimes in the past, she had imagined what it would be like if Blake made love to her—of course she had. But the reality was nothing like the dream. The reality was harsh, brutal, and dimly she knew she should be resisting, while her treacherous body moved beneath his in a frenzy of pleasure that made her moan and cry out as with a final long, shuddering sigh she lay limp and motionless, drained of sensation, drugged with fulfilment.

Maggie couldn't remember when she had had a full night's sleep, but tonight she slept without consciousness of dreaming and wakened to see sunshine edging the heavy curtains.

Blake was lying on his side, turned towards her, one arm flung out sideways. He was sleeping heavily, breathing deeply and evenly, and she lay beside him remembering last night with a sensual happiness, her limbs warm and relaxed under the light bedcover.

She propped herself up on one elbow and studied his face. All the anger was smoothed out of it; he looked younger and somehow he seemed curiously uncertain and vulnerable. A lock of dark hair straggled across his forehead and the dark shadow on his chin merged with the thicker line of hair that grew straight down his chest. Her pulses quickened, remembering how she had clung to him, remembering the roughness of his springy hair against her flesh.

She wanted to stretch out a hand and touch him. If he wakened now what would happen? Would he be glad to find her in bed beside him—roused, perhaps, to want her again? Or would he turn away from her coldly, hating her because she wasn't Fiona?

She couldn't risk it. Silently she slid out of bed and crossed to the shower-room, her bare feet making no sound on the thick carpet. She dressed in a white cotton dress with a demure frill round the neckline and hem. She wanted something as different as possible from the scarlet dress she had worn last night. Blake should have no excuse for calling her a tart this morning, she thought with a flash of angry resentment. She was painfully conscious of him sleeping in the bed behind her as she brushed her curly brown hair and put on a light make-up. When she had finished she walked over and stood beside the bed, looking down on this man who had the power to cause her so much pain and give her so much ecstasy. She stood there for minutes, but he didn't stir, and finally she went out of the room and closed the door quietly.

The staff of Mordens usually gathered in one of the

hotel restaurants for breakfast, but today Maggie avoided that particular place and found a small snack-bar serving coffee and rolls. She sat down at a table in a corner and hoped she wouldn't be noticed.

Vain hope! Almost before she had settled down she saw Nick coming across to her. He stopped beside the table, with a quick look over his shoulder. 'Are you on your own?' The worry lines between his fair brows were deeper than usual this morning.

When she nodded he slipped into a chair beside her. 'Maggie—my dear girl, what a thing to happen last night! I couldn't go into the office this morning until I'd reassured myself that things were O.K. between you and Blake. I wouldn't for the world be the cause of any trouble. The poor old chap *was* in a state—all that commuting backwards and forwards—he must have been in the final stages of jet-lag. I don't wonder he got all mixed up and jumped to conclusions.'

He was trying to take the sting out of a nasty little episode, but under the half-joking words she could sense his uneasiness. She answered in a matter-of-fact tone, 'I think you're right, Nick. He was dead tired, absolutely good for nothing at all.' *Nothing at all?* She felt her cheeks go warm and bent her head lower over her coffee cup. 'I'm sure he'll see things more clearly this morning after a good night's sleep.'

He looked a little doubtfully at her. 'I hope so, indeed. But if there *was* gossip that reached him about you and me I think I know where it started from.'

'I think we both do,' Maggie said, and their eyes met in confirmation.

Nick pursed his lips. 'She's a difficult girl, with an outsize inferiority complex. I took her out a couple of times in London last year. It sounds rather patronising, but I suppose I was sorry for her, and I was feeling very sorry for myself too at that time. I had to pull out when I found she was building too much on it. I tried to do it kindly, but she didn't take it kindly, I'm afraid.'

He sighed and Maggie looked at him with a little smile. 'You're too softhearted altogether, Nick. You were being kind to me too, this last week, weren't you?'

He pulled a wry face at her. 'That,' he said, 'was something altogether different. I did it far more for myself than for you, Maggie, as I think you're aware, but we won't go into all that again. You know how I feel, but I'm sure I ought to fade out of the picture completely from now on. I wouldn't for the world be the cause of any trouble between you and Blake, however unjustified it might be.' He stood up and put a hand lightly on her shoulder. 'Back to the grindstone now, I suppose. We'll be meeting in the course of business, I expect. All the best, Maggie.'

She watched him walk away. Nick was the dearest of men, but never in this world could he rouse her to the kind of frenzy that Blake had roused her to last night. It was true what they said, she thought ruefully, it was the difficult, arrogant, demanding men who sent women crazy for them. It didn't seem fair.

She turned back to the table and as her eyes wandered round the room her heart gave a great lurch and started to thump with heavy beats. Blake was standing just inside the entrance opposite to the one by which Nick had left. He must have dressed hastily, for his shirt was buttoned unevenly and there was a short gash on his jaw where he had managed to cut himself.

He came across and took the chair that Nick had just vacated. 'So,' he sneered, 'you couldn't wait to get together again, could you?'

Maggie didn't reply. She got up and procured another cup of coffee—black—and set it before him. 'Drink that up and don't be silly, Blake,' she said. 'Of course Nick wanted to make sure that you weren't still playing the jealous husband.'

'And did you manage to put his mind at rest?' He took a gulp of coffee and shot her a suspicious look. 'Or did you tell him our marriage was a put-up job?'

'No, of course I didn't. I knew you'd see things differently when you thought about it. You were in no mood to think clearly last night.' She met his eyes levelly. 'You didn't really believe that I would start some sort of affair with Nick Grant, when I'd just married you? Surely you know me better than that.'

She spoke in the tone she had always used when they were together. Reasonable, friendly, not the slightest hint of sexual challenge. She was giving him a chance to get back on their old terms, to agree tacitly that last night had been a kind of madness, born of anger and the tiredness that clouds one's power of thought.

Blake was holding his coffee cup in both hands, watching her over its rim, and something in his eyes made her rush on nervously, 'I've been going into the office each day while you've been away and I think I'm getting the hang of things there. I've also met some of our Chinese colleagues. Shall we go in this morning and go through a few things together? If you're rested, that is,' she finished rather lamely.

He had his sardonic expression now. '*I* shall go into the office. You won't.'

That took her by surprise. 'W-why not?' she stammered.

'Because I say you won't.' This was Blake at his most arrogant. 'I don't want you working with me any longer.

From now on you'll be here simply as my wife.'

'But you said—you said——' Maggie felt stunned '—that was why you asked me to marry you. You said—so that I could come out here with you and go on being your assistant.'

He put down his cup and shrugged. 'At that time I said a lot of things that didn't make any sort of sense later. We all make mistakes sometimes.'

'Then——' she faltered, 'it hardly seems worthwhile my staying in Hong Kong, does it? Perhaps you'd like me to go home. You could make some excuse—illness or something.'

'No,' he said sharply. 'You'll stay here and go on being my wife—so far as the staff here are concerned anyway.' He smiled thinly. 'I think I can promise you that there won't be a repeat performance of last night's Othello scene. As you so rightly said——' he raised dark brows cynically, '—I was in no fit state to see sweet reason.'

'Then you do believe that I wasn't having an affair with Nick?'

'Oh yes, I believe you. I have to, don't I? I was given unassailable proof.'

She felt her cheeks begin to burn and could say nothing.

Blake leaned back in his chair and his eyes moved slowly over her crimson cheeks down her neck to the hint of cleavage showing beneath the demure white collar. 'But I must say you surprised me,' he went on. 'I wouldn't have believed the cool, efficient Maggie could have responded like that. For a shy, unawakened virgin you were terrific.' His voice was loaded with irony.

'That was—it didn't mean that I was in love with you,' she whispered hoarsely, glancing round the room to see if anyone could overhear this extraordinary conversation, 'Any more than it meant you were in love with me,' she added, because somehow a tiny bit of pride must be salvaged out of this wretched situation. She wondered fleetingly how he would react if she said, 'It meant that I was crazy for you, in every possible way. Not only to sleep with you, but to live with you, work for you, make you happy, share things. It meant that you are the centre of my life and that without you my life would be a barren desert.'

Blake looked faintly amused. 'What would you call it, then? Just good old-fashioned lust?'

'Something like that,' Maggie muttered, turning her head away. She was painfully aware of his scrutiny and couldn't bear to see the look of amusement in his eyes. Making love to her last night had meant nothing to him—he had been roused by anger and frustration and probably he had closed his eyes and pretended it was Fiona there in the bed with him. That was the worst of all. Maggie bit her lip hard, groping desperately for some way to change the subject.

'Let's get this straight,' she said slowly. 'You want me to stay in Hong Kong, acting as your wife?'

He nodded. 'Right first time.'

'Just for the look of it?'

'Exactly—for the look of it. There's no better way to kill gossip than to demonstrate that it's untrue and unfounded. And I intend that this particular bit of gossip shall be well and truly killed forthwith.'

There was a silence. He was looking across the table at her with an expression she didn't recognise. Almost she could imagine that she saw pleading in his face.

But of course—the work! The opportunity to carry off this huge complex assignment in triumph meant everything to him. Everything, that was, except having Fiona out here with him. He couldn't have Fiona while he was still married to her, Maggie, so he intended to make the best of a bad job.

She crumbled her roll between her fingers nervously. 'So,' she said, 'I'm to stay with you and act the loving wife to boost your reputation with the company and to prevent any sinister stories reaching J.M. back in London?'

'Correct!' he said crisply. 'Would it be so difficult?' He gave her a narrow, meaningful look that sent shivers coursing up and down her spine.

'If you're suggesting what I think you are, it would be impossible,' said Maggie, lifting her chin a little. 'Last night must be considered a one-off, as far as I'm concerned.'

Blake raised dark brows sceptically. He must think, after the way she had behaved last night, that she wouldn't be able to refuse him anything. Well, she would show him that he was wrong. 'Really?' he said.

'Yes, really,' snapped Maggie.

He shrugged. 'Seems a pity,' he said indifferently, 'but if that's the way you want it——'

'That *is* the way I want it,' Maggie said coldly.

'As you wish, then.' He sounded as if he didn't care either way, and probably he didn't. He would take her if she was willing, but he wasn't going to shed tears over it if she wasn't. How little she had really known about him, she thought suddenly. And how differently a man could behave in his private life from the way he was at work!

She kept her voice steady as she asked, 'And how long will this charade go on?'

He shrugged. 'As long as it takes.'

She wanted to scream at him, As long as *what* takes? Did he mean the work here, or did he mean as long as it took to arrange a divorce in the usual way, as an annulment was apparently out of the question?

She said, 'I think a divorce takes two years, if both parties are agreeable, isn't that right?'

'I believe so.'

She swallowed hard. She couldn't help it—she had to ask. 'And will Fiona wait that long for you?'

'We won't discuss Fiona,' he said crushingly. And that was that.

There was a strained silence between them while the noisy, morning clatter and chatter in the snack-bar rose and fell. At last Maggie said quietly, 'Very well, Blake, I agree, for the sake of the Company and the work out here. Although I don't know what on earth I'm going to do to fill my time.'

He was on his feet immediately. That, at least, was like the old Blake. Once he had gained his point he couldn't wait to put things in motion.

'Oh, you'll find something—gang up with some of the other wives,' he said carelessly. 'Now, I'll get along to the office. I'll meet you back here in our suite at around five and we'll make arrangements about money and so on. You'll have your own bank account, of course.'

He glanced around. Two of Morden's girl secretaries were sitting a few tables away. 'Be seeing you, sweetheart,' he said quite loudly. 'Be good.' He leaned down and kissed Maggie full on her lips. When he lifted his head he smiled into her eyes, lingering as if he couldn't bear to drag himself away from her. Then he turned and walked out of the room, leaving her speechless at the speed with which everything had happened and weak at the knees as her lips tingled from his kiss. There had been no makebelieve about that kiss, and it left her wondering how she was going to stop herself going up in flames again. Blake would believe she was available for his casual lovemaking, and despise her for it while accepting what she was prepared to offer. She shivered, feeling cheap and humiliated. Perhaps she should have insisted on going back home and letting the staff of Mordens make what they liked of it. But she had promised——

She drank another cup of coffee and then went up in the lift to the suite she was sharing with Blake. One largish living room with a view over the harbour, one bedroom, a shower-room and a tiny sliver of kitchen which, under different circumstances, would have delighted Maggie, with its miniature sink, its electric kettle and small microwave oven. If things had been right between them she could easily have cooked a passable meal here and they could have eaten cosily together if they hadn't wanted to go out. She was sure that Blake would come in from work every evening tired and hungry. The way he pushed himself was alarming. When the job demanded it he thought nothing of working all night and into the following day. If she had been a real wife, she thought forlornly, she could have looked after him. Unobtrusively, of course, because Blake hated to be fussed over. Tactfully, the way she had done back in England. Just keeping an eye on him and making sure he got enough food and enough sleep to safeguard his health.

Sleep. The word brought her up short. She stared at the big double bed and her insides began to churn as she remembered how it had been last night, with Blake's arms holding her, remembered how he had looked in sleep when she had left him this morning, his dark hair tousled against the whiteness of the pillow. The chambermaid must have been up here already, for the bed was tidied now to a smooth, perfect plumpness. It was a wide bed, a honeymoon bed. But this wasn't a honeymoon, and Blake was going to have to sleep somewhere else.

There was a long sofa in the living room. One of them could sleep on that; they'd have to work it out, she thought, trying to be cool and rational about it. She supposed it wouldn't do for Blake to book another room for himself. All the staff of Mordens were being accommodated in this hotel and sooner or later the word would get around that the gossip had been right after all: Blake Morden's new marriage was already on the rocks.

Maggie turned away. She couldn't bear to stand here any longer looking at that bed. She went back into the living room and stood gazing down at the harbour far below with its busy craft plying ceaselessly to and fro. She leaned her forehead against the glass, already warm with the morning sunshine, and tried to adjust to the new situation she found herself in. Maggie was a worker, always had been, and the thought of staying here in this luxury palace of a hotel with nothing definite to fill her time appalled her.

At home, on the rare occasions when she didn't go in to work, she would have rung up one of her married friends, arranged a game of tennis or a trip to the swimming baths, or just to meet for a coffee. But here there were no friends to turn to. Then she remembered Ling San. Ling San was a darling, full of life and enthusiasm, and that was just what she needed. Maggie found her notebook and rang Ling San's number.

Ling San answered immediately. 'Maggie—how

lucky, you've just caught me. I was on my way out.' The light voice with its charming American intonation was enough to raise Maggie's spirits several notches. 'I have such news for you! Dietrich has found me a little shop and I am just going there to start arranging it for my beauty bazaar. It is in the arcade of your hotel. Will you come and see it with me?'

Maggie had wandered along the hotel shopping arcade several times, during the week she had been on her own, and found it fascinating, with its windows stacked with luxury goods. There were tailors' premises, where a suit could be made to measure in less than forty-eight hours; shops showing jade and ivory carvings; others with fabulous carpets from all over the world. China—jewellery—electronic goods—everything.

Ling San's proposed shop was long and narrow, tucked away between mink coats on one side and fashion shoes on the other.

'Come in and we will explore.' Ling San fitted a key in the lock. 'Oh look, it is perfect for me. See, there is even a shampoo bay, with bowls and water and everything. Oh, I shall do so well here!' She danced around, a neat little figure with her smooth raven-dark hair a shining cap and her pale coffee cheeks flushed with excitement, poking into corners, inspecting everything, deciding where to place her own tables and stands. She was wearing a pure silk shift in a subtle shade of dusty pink, simply and perfectly cut to show off her delicate curves. She looked, Maggie thought, like a tiny ballerina. When she had vetted every corner of the shop she pronounced it perfect for her needs. Later, over a coffee, she said to Maggie, 'I shall start to fit it up straight away. It will be fun.' She sighed. 'What a pity you are so busy building things, Maggie, or I should ask you to help me.'

'But I'm not,' said Maggie. 'Blake has come back from the U.K. with the news that the Chairman, his father, doesn't think it would be quite "on" for his son's wife to work for the Corporation.' That was twisting the truth a little, but the fact remained the same. 'So I'm at a loose end just now and not enjoying it very much. I like to be busy. If there's anything I can do, I'd love to help.'

Ling San clapped her hands delightedly. 'Oh, that is wonderful! We shall work so well together, I know it. And the shop will be such a success. Of course there are many other beauty parlours in Hong Kong, some even in this hotel, but ours will be quite different. Do you know what I mean to call it? Don't laugh. I shall call it Nu Yu.' She spelled it out. 'What do you think of that? It sounds a little Chinese, but do you see the joke?'

Maggie creased her forehead. 'Nu Yu?' Then she grinned. 'Yes, of course—New You. That's super, Ling San. You'll make a new image for women who are tired of their old one.'

'Yes, that is right. What do you think?' Ling San put her little dark head on one side.

'I think it's a brainwave and I can't wait to get started. Can we do anything straight away? Today?' Maggie could almost feel her old drive and vitality flowing back into her at the prospect of being involved in an interesting plan. She hadn't quite realised until this moment how the last few weeks had drained her of the liveliness that she had always taken for granted. Blake's decision that she should not be working with him here had seemed the last straw. But now she felt that if she were involved with Ling San in this new venture it would make life at the very least bearable.

'Sure,' Ling San sparkled. 'We will go along and see Dietrich at his bank and tell him that the shop is splendid and that he must rent it for me and then we can begin to plan. Come along, Maggie.' Ling San jumped up and held out her hand, her dark eyes alight, and Maggie, infected by the Chinese girl's gaiety, followed her out of the coffee-shop, feeling that once again life might have some purpose. At least, if she were involved in this project with Ling San she wouldn't be dependent upon Blake's every mood.

Almost, she felt, she might one day be free of this consuming love that had brought her so much unhappiness.

The day, which had begun so disastrously, got better as it went on. Dietrich Hauser was obviously pleased and intrigued with his pretty wife's enthusiastic plans. Urged on by Ling San, he left his impressive office at the bank to finalise the details of the lease. When this was done he took the two girls to lunch at a garden restaurant in the hotel, where they ate Dim Sum. This turned out to be a selection of spicy snacks—a sort of Chinese hors d'œuvres. Maggie wasn't yet completely at home with chopsticks and her efforts amused the other two vastly. They were laughing at her expense when Nick Grant appeared at the entrance to the restaurant and stood looking around.

He spotted the three of them immediately and came over to their table. 'Well met, you people. Am I allowed to join the party?' He took their consent for granted and sat down beside Maggie. 'How's everyone?'

Ling San immediately embarked on her news. 'Nick, you must know, I am now a professional woman. Is that not so, my darling?' she appealed to Dietrich.

'She's correct,' said the young German with a grin. He scratched his blond head ruefully. 'She has rushed me off my feet, my friend, and is about to ask for a large loan from my bank—I know it.'

Ling San pulled a face at him. 'All business women need loans, is it not so?' she appealed to Nick. 'Maggie has promised to help me with setting up my shop,' she added.

Nick frowned. 'I thought——'

Maggie didn't let him finish. 'Blake has made me redundant,' she grinned. 'He thinks the wife of the Chairman's son shouldn't be seen slaving away on a building site.'

'And you don't mind?' Nick was looking at her intently. He knew how much her work had always meant to her.

'Oh, I think he's probably right,' she said airily. 'And I shall have great fun helping Ling San.'

'Well, if it's what you want,' Nick shrugged, 'that's fine. When do we see the new venture?'

'As soon as it's all furnished and ready to open,' Ling San told him. 'We shall have a grand opening party to celebrate, and you're invited, of course, Nick.'

He accepted eagerly, and Maggie thought that Blake wasn't going to be pleased when he found that she was involved with Nick again, even in a distant way, through mutual friends. Then she thought, Well, what does it matter? Blake doesn't own me. And her new confidence began to emerge again.

Hours later the two girls were sitting on the floor of the empty shop, surrounded by drawings and plans jotted down on odd scraps of paper. Ling San hugged her knees, her eyes very bright. 'That's it for today, Maggie.

What do you think of it, so far?'

Maggie hugged her knees. 'I think you're wonderful, Ling San. You know it all!'

The Chinese girl laughed. 'That's not so wonderful. I was trained in New York, where my aunt lives, and I worked at a very famous beautician's there for almost three years. Then Dietrich and I were married and we came back to live in Hong Kong. I was happy to come back because my parents live here. They sent me to New York to be trained, but all the time I dreamed of starting my own business here. So you see, it has been a dream for a long time.'

'And sometimes dreams come true,' sighed Maggie.

'Yes, sometimes, if one dreams long enough,' Ling San agreed. She looked rather hard at Maggie as they scrambled to their feet. 'Your dreams have come true too, Maggie,' she said a little shyly. 'You have married a wonderful man. I look forward to meeting him.'

'As soon as it can be aranged,' Maggie promised. Blake should be pleased that she had found herself an interesting occupation. He could get on with his own work and needn't spare her more than a passing thought now and then. That was what he wanted, wasn't it? she thought bitterly, and sadness overtook her again. But she thrust it away quickly and looked at her watch. 'Good heavens, it's half-past five and I arranged to meet Blake at five o'clock. See you tomorrow morning, Ling San.' She hurried away along the arcade and found a lift to whisk her up to the twenty-third floor.

The door was unlocked and Blake was stretched out in a deep armchair, a whisky beside him, a dark look on his face.

'Where the hell have you been?' he greeted her. 'I was on the point of going out to look for you. I thought I said we'd meet at five o'clock.'

'Did you? I don't remember.' Maggie sank into the depths of the sofa, opposite. 'Afraid I didn't notice the time. Will you pour me a drink, please? Bitter lemon.'

He shot her a suspicious glance. 'You're very pleased with yourself, all of a sudden,' he said sourly. 'Where have you been?'

'Oh, round and about,' she said airily, holding out a hand for her drink. 'I'm beginning to get quite fond of Hong Kong. There's so much going on all the time here.'

'What, for instance?'

She lifted her eyebrows. 'What do you mean—what?'

'I mean what's been going on today that makes you look so jaunty?' He took a sip of his drink. 'Surely I may be allowed to take an interest in my wife's activities?'

That took Maggie aback, but she said amiably, 'Why, of course, Blake.' She grinned. 'I didn't think you cared.' She was inviting him to share a joke as they had once done—in another life, it seemed.

He didn't smile back. 'I want to make sure you haven't been with Nick Grant. I happen to know he was missing from his office for a considerable time in the middle of the day.'

Maggie sighed. 'Oh, Blake dear, you *have* got a nasty suspicious mind! What on earth did you imagine Nick and I could be doing in the middle of the day?'

'I can imagine all sorts of things you might be doing. Now I've had a demonstration of your talents,' he drawled, his eyes passing over her with a long, assessing look.

She flushed deeply. 'That's a rotten thing to say, Blake. I thought we'd left that particular subject behind for good.'

'The subject of your talents in bed? Oh no, my dear, that's not a subject a man ever leaves behind, don't you know that?' He was looking at her in a way that sent a spasm of something like fear clutching at her inside.

He stood up and deliberately took the empty glass from her fingers. 'You've finished your drink, I see. Now—how would you suggest we spend the time until dinner?'

She looked away from his narrowed gaze that held an unmistakable meaning, and her heart began to throb with slow, suffocating beats. 'I d-don't know. I—I thought——'

'Don't think,' he said softly. He lowered himself beside her on to the sofa and slid an arm round her waist, drawing her against him. 'Thinking is a bad habit at a time like this.' He pressed his cheek against her hair, nuzzling her ear gently. 'Maggie?' he whispered.

She was tense all over as if an electric current had passed through her body, transfixing her. His hand was on her neck now, pushing away the thin cotton dress and stroking the smooth skin of her shoulder. Then he drew one finger down to her breast with a sensual, arousing touch that sent shivers of pleasure along her nerves.

'Relax, sweetheart.' Blake's voice came huskily at her ear. 'We're so good together—remember?'

He pushed her down gently, drawing away a little to unfasten the buttons at the front of her dress. She was swimming in a great warm wave of longing. In another moment she would reach up and pull him down to her. His fingers touched her skin lightly as he unfastened the buttons one by one, neatly and expertly. 'Wouldn't a zipp be more practical?' he said, in an amused voice.

Maggie never knew exactly why, but suddenly, at his words, a great revulsion of feeling overcame her. It was as if she stepped outside herself and saw the two of them lying there on the sofa. This had happened so many times before for Blake, with so many different girls. Probably he had said the very same words. He was a past-master in the art of lovemaking, he knew exactly the technique to get what he wanted from a girl.

But something inside Maggie was screaming, I need more than that—to be one of the women he has made love to. I want something lasting—something special. I want his love, not just to be an object of desire.

'No!' she gasped, pushing him away with all her strength and dragging herself upright, fumbling with shaking fingers to close the front of her dress. 'No—I don't want this—I told you. You promised!' she almost shouted as she saw his face darken and he reached out for her.

She slid from his grasp and stumbled across the room, standing with her back to the bedroom door as if she were guarding it against invasion—which, perhaps, she was.

Blake stood up, straightening his jacket. It was amazing how quickly he got possession of himself. He strolled to the drinks cabinet and refilled his glass. 'O.K., O.K.,' he said shortly, 'there's no need to get worked up about it. I merely thought we might attempt to close the breach between us, and I know of no better way. But if you don't want to, you don't. I'm not going to force myself on you.'

It was extraordinary—she was capable of hurting his masculine pride, it seemed. She should have felt triumph, but instead she was conscious of a queer sense of remorse.

She went across and touched his arm. 'I want to close the breach too, Blake, you must know that. But I expect a woman's way is different from a man's,' she added in her practical voice.

He stood looking down at her for a long moment. Then he put a finger under her chin and tipped her head back. 'Funny little Maggie, you don't change, do you?' he said softly. Incredibly, he smiled and her heart seemed to miss a beat. It was so long since she had seen him smile. 'Perhaps we've been taking all this too seriously,' he said. 'We've been making a great big drama of it, both of us. Perhaps the time has come to draw back a bit and take things as they come. What do you think, Maggie, shall we call a truce?'

She wanted to laugh aloud and throw her arms round his neck. Instead she said quietly, 'I think, Blake, that that's a very good idea.'

He went on looking at her, his face suddenly quizzical. Then he said briskly, 'Good. Well then, suppose you start by telling me how your day went?'

CHAPTER SEVEN

THIS was what she had wanted, she told herself, swallowing a quite unreasonable twinge of disappointment. To be on their old terms of easy friendship was all she could expect. She must somehow manage to forget that Blake had held her in his arms, had roused her to a pitch of passion she had never thought herself capable of. She mustn't let herself remember, and yearn for him or the situation would become impossible.

So she put a bright smile on her lips and began, 'Well, there's this Hong Kong Chinese girl I met in Macau, Ling San, and she's starting her own beauty shop in the hotel arcade and——'

Blake listened with apparent interest, putting in a question here and there. When she had finished he said, 'It sounds quite a good proposition. Although I can't quite see you in a beauty shop, Maggie.'

She pulled a face at him. 'Why not?'

He put out a hand and tweaked a brown curl, as he had done many times before when they had laughed and teased each other. 'I suppose because I'm used to seeing you on a building site in jeans and windcheater. Or in the office in a businesslike trouser suit.'

'Oh, people can change,' she said lightly.

He looked down at her with an expression she couldn't interpret. 'Yes,' he said, 'people can change.' Then he began to talk about something else almost immediately and she had to make what she could of that remark.

That conversation set the tone of their relationship in the next weeks. Blake was friendly but enigmatic and Maggie didn't dare question him, although she longed to ask about Fiona, about what he had in mind for the future of their marriage, whether he intended to get a divorce when the time came. Blake didn't ask any questions about her feelings or proffer any information about his own. It was a truce, but with no real understanding. An armed truce, it could be called.

Never did he attempt to make love to her again, and only in the presence of one of the office staff did he touch her or kiss her. At night he took it for granted that he should sleep on the sofa in the big lounge room of their suite. He was punctiliously polite about sharing the shower-room, and grateful for any small chore she performed for him, like sewing on a button or washing through a pair of socks or a thin shirt when he needed something quickly.

They might, Maggie thought, almost have been brother and sister.

And of course he never knew of the sleepless hours that she spent tossing alone in the big bed, breaking all her good resolutions about not remembering how it had been when they had shared it, walking up and down silently on the soft carpet, half crazy with her need for him. Only the thought of his contemptuous acceptance of her stopped her from opening the door that divided them.

Then one night he disappeared—she heard the door close behind him—and didn't return until early morning. Lying wide awake, shivering in the cool of the air-conditioning, Maggie drew her own conclusions about where he had been. She knew all about the topless bars and night-clubs of Hong Kong.

After that it was a little easier for her to sleep at night. She only had to remind herself that Blake didn't change—if he couldn't have Fiona, then any girl would do.

She saw hardly anything of him from the time he left after breakfast until he returned in the evening, hot and tired, and staggered into the shower-room. He was totally immersed in the job now. Maggie couldn't resist asking the odd question about it now and again and he answered quite readily, even going into some of the details that she would be familiar with—matters that they had been working on together before they came out here. One day he took her out to the site in the New Territories and she watched the great earth-moving machines at work.

It was awesome to think they could carve off the top of a hill and drop it into the water and then build on it. 'It's absolutely fascinating,' she breathed. 'I know it was all worked out and it's been done over and over again in Hong Kong, but somehow I never quite believed it was possible until this moment.'

She turned to Blake, her eyes shining, and he smiled down at her. 'Missing being in on the action?' he queried. 'Isn't the beauty shop a good substitute?'

'Oh, I'm quite happy,' she replied quickly. Blake

wasn't going to be allowed to guess how much his rejection had hurt her.

He said quietly. 'It was J.M.'s decision, you know, not mine, that you should stop working with me. He thought I needed you more as a wife than as an assistant.' He didn't give her time to make any reply, if, indeed she could have thought of one. He took her arm. 'Now, come along, I want to show you my headquarters.'

As she went with him she was aware of a warmth spreading through her that had nothing to do with the hot, humid atmosphere of the place. So it hadn't been Blake's decision to get her out of her job after all. It hadn't been that he didn't want her working with him. That was a real consolation, another tiny boost to her confidence.

Helping Ling San to set up her beauty shop was a new experience for Maggie. Sometimes she stopped and looked at her reflection in one of the long mirrors framed in silver filigree and hardly knew herself. The long-legged tomboy who had played on equal terms with her three brothers, the jeans-and-sweater student who had turned into a capable woman engineer, was now engaged in the business of glamour, of lotions and creams and face-masks, of mascara and eye-shadows, of powders and blushers and lipsticks, in such a bewildering range of colour and texture that Maggie's head spun as she aranged them on the rose-tinted glass tops of the cabinets.

But Ling San knew exactly what she wanted. 'And you, my dear Maggie, will be my guinea-pig,' she announced, her little head on one side, her dark eyes full of fun. 'That does not sound very flattering, but wait until you see what I shall do to you. I have got a little out of practice since I left New York,' she explained as she pushed Maggie into one of the new treatment couches, upholstered in soft amethyst leather. 'I must see if I can get my touch back.'

Maggie submitted, relaxing happily as Ling San's cool expert fingers massaged her face and neck with soothing strokes. 'It is quite a pity,' the Chinese girl lamented, 'that you have such a beautiful skin to begin with. There is nothing to work a miracle upon because the miracle is already there, but at least we can experiment to find the perfect make-up for you.'

And experiment she did. 'A warm, glowing look for day-time,' she mused, 'emphasising your lip colour. You have such a tempting mouth, Maggie. So generous, so inviting.'

Maggie felt the colour rising to her cheeks. 'I always thought it was too large,' she mumbled, but Ling San shook her head decisively.

'It is a mouth a man would fall in love with,' she announced with all the assurance of a professional in such matters, and Maggie knew better than to argue. It wasn't true, of course. Blake had certainly not fallen in love with her mouth. Then her pulses quickened as she felt again the probing touch of his lips on hers, forcing her mouth to open to his kiss. With an effort she tried to concentrate on what Ling San was saying.

'And for evenings,' the Chinese girl mused, 'mysterious, romantic, dreamy.'

Ling San was in her element. She smoothed and patted and brushed, standing back to assess the results like an artist with his picture, chatting away to herself as she worked. 'Just the lightest dusting of powder over the foundation, a touch of shimmering blusher high on the cheeks here—and here. You have very beautiful bone-structure, Maggie. And your eyes—yes, a bronze shadow, I think, to make them glow like those lovely velvety wallflowers you grow in English gardens. There, I am getting quite poetic!'

The results of the experiments sometimes astonished Maggie and sometimes gave her a heady sense of elation. But always, before she left in the evening, the exotic make-ups were carefully removed; that was her one condition. If she were going to confront Blake with a new Maggie (and she hadn't quite made up her mind about this yet) then everything must be right for the occasion. 'He's used to me looking ordinary,' she said to Ling San. 'I don't know whether he's going to take to my glamorous image.'

Ling San argued, 'All men like their women to look glamorous, my dear Maggie, and I'm sure your Blake is no different.'

Maggie agreed inwardly that that was probably true. Blake's girl-friends had all been lovelies, and she had never imagined she could compete. But now, under Ling San's clever hands, she began to wonder if perhaps she could.

It was over a month before Ling San's beauty shop was ready to open, but finally the time arrived. Every last pot and bottle and packet and tube had been delivered and stocked. The very latest equipment had been installed. The whole shop, with its décor of amethyst shading to pale shell-pink, glowed with a muted, chic appeal. Here, rich women would come to be cosseted and pandered to, and sent out looking even more polished and urbane, fashionable and elegant than when they came in.

As the day approached for the opening party Maggie became more and more undecided. Should she buy a romantic dress, let Ling San get to work on her, and if she did, would Blake be impressed—or indifferent—or even angry? She didn't know. She never had the least idea what Blake was thinking these days. On the surface their relationship was amicable, but it frightened her even to guess what lay below the surface.

'Have you asked Blake if Wednesday is O.K. for him?' Ling San asked Maggie. 'I know how busy he is, but we *must* choose a time when he can come to the party. I cannot wait to see his face when he sees his new wife!'

'Ling San, I'm not quite sure——' began Maggie, but the Chinese girl was poring over her list of guests, biting the end of her pencil. 'Dietrich will bring many of his rich clients,' she said. 'He has promised. And they will bring their elegant wives. And you will look more elegant than any of them, Maggie. They will wonder who it was that did your hair and chose your make-up and they will guess, and I shall have a long, long queue waiting the next morning.' She laughed gaily. 'Well, it may not be quite like that, but there is no harm in hoping. Now, let us talk about your dress, Maggie.'

Maggie smiled and sighed and gave in. She couldn't tell Ling San about her doubts. They had had such fun together, and Ling San was so innocently pleased with her plan for a transformed Maggie, that it would be too unkind to refuse. 'I was wondering if you would come with me and help me choose,' she said, and was rewarded by Ling San's beaming smile.

'I so hoped you would ask me,' she confessed. 'Let us go this afternoon. We will look at all the boutiques and all the big department stores and have a lot of fun.'

Maggie agreed. 'Just so long as you don't want me to wear scarlet,' she said.

'Scarlet? You?' Ling San screamed in horror. 'Never in this world! It would not suit you at all. But why do you say no scarlet, though?' She lifted her pencil-thin eyebrows.

'Blake doesn't like it,' said Maggie wryly, and Ling San asked no more questions. She had often told Maggie that she believed that wives should dress to please their husbands, which meant that they should look their most appealing selves.

That evening, over dinner at their usual restaurant, Maggie asked Blake about the party.

'Oh lord, must I?' he groaned. 'I've got a hell of a lot of paper work to get through in the next couple of weeks.'

'Ling San will be terribly disappointed if you don't come,' Maggie said, adding with a sideways grin, 'She's taken quite a fancy to you, it seems.'

Maggie and Blake had dined with the Hausers, at their luxurious apartment high up on Victoria Peak, one evening soon after Maggie had started to work with Ling San, and the occasion had been quite a success. The two men had got on well together, talking business until Ling San put a stop to it by insisting that Blake and Maggie should learn to play mah-jongg. Blake had approved of Ling San too. 'She's like a Chinese work of art,' he said in his amused voice. 'Quite exquisite, and very feminine.'

'I'm glad you like her,' Maggie said brightly. It hurt a little to think that never in this world would he describe *her* in those words. She was 'Maggie' again now. Good old Maggie. Maggie the reliable friend. Maggie the colleague with whom he was once again talking over his problems at work. She wondered bleakly if he had ever seen her as a desirable woman at all, not even on the night he made love to her and drew a passionate response from her. That was all in the past. Now he was looking elsewhere for his women, she supposed, as he had disappeared every night this last week and only come back in time for breakfast, without making an excuse or offering an explanation for his absence.

It wouldn't go on long like this between them, Maggie thought. It *couldn't*. Soon now, they would have to talk it out and make some plan for their future. Whatever Blake himself wanted, she didn't think she could go on living this way, a wife and yet not a wife.

And there was something else too. She hadn't faced it yet; she hadn't even tried to imagine how it would affect the situation if she were actually pregnant. It was a huge, awesome possibility that got more and more like a probability as each day passed. Maggie couldn't allow herself to believe it yet. More than anything she longed to have Blake's baby. But how Blake himself would view the prospect was an unknown quantity. There was just one thing about which she had already made up her mind in advance. Nothing and nobody—not even Blake himself—would persuade her to get rid of Blake's child.

The day of the opening party arrived. Blake had gone off very early to the building site in the New Territories. 'I'll make it if I can,' he had promised vaguely. 'But don't expect me to be on time. I have to go into the office when I get back.'

It had been arranged that the guests should assemble in the salon. There they would drink champagne and toast the success of the new venture. After that they would all repair to the hotel's most exclusive restaurant for dinner, arrangements for which had been made in advance. There would be almost fifty invited guests and Maggie thought that it was going to cost Dietrich a pretty penny, but he seemed quite oblivious of the expense. It was enough that his adored little wife wanted it. Ling San basked in his loving generosity and showed,

whenever they were together, that she returned his ador-
ation. Lucky couple, Maggie thought wisfully.

Ling San was very excited, although obviously trying
to appear calm. 'You will come to our apartment to
dress,' she told Maggie. 'Blake must not see you until
just the right moment. Then his eyes will open wide,
you will see.'

'I hope you're right,' said Maggie with a wry smile.
But she fell in with all Ling San's plans. She had gone
too far now to back out, and she knew that Ling San
would be desperately disappointed if she did.

The afternoon was spent in the salon, elegant in its
décor of amethyst, with masses of shell-pink rosebuds
backed by feathery fern in pure white ceramic bowls,
intricately decorated with Chinese handwork.

The door was securely locked and the blinds drawn
while Ling San performed her magic on Maggie's hair.
The thick brown curls fell to the floor as she snipped
and trimmed. There were lotions and conditioners, and
periods spent with the shining new electronically-
operated machines that thought for themselves. Maggie
had ceased to worry about the result as she drowsed her
way through the stages of the transformation in a warm,
perfumed haze.

At last, triumphantly, Ling San said, 'There—how do
you like it?'

As she spun the chair round, Maggie saw her reflection. For a moment she was speechless. 'It's—it's—I
can't believe it's me!'

'The new you, of course,' Ling San reminded her with
a gratified little smile. 'My very first work of art, don't
you agree, Maggie?'

Maggie stared into the mirror. The curly-haired
tomboy image had gone for good. In its place was an

elegant young woman of fashion. The curls had been cut and shaped to form curves that clung to her head, emphasising its pretty shape, which had never showed to advantage before. Her face looked different too, thinner and more interesting as the fronds of soft, gleaming hair slanted towards her cheekbones, throwing the hollows of her cheeks into faint shadow.

She met Ling San's eyes in the mirror and shook her head in amazement. 'You're a genius, Ling San. I hardly recognised myself. I never knew a hair-style could make so much difference.'

'You really like it?'

'Oh yes, indeed I do. I'm thrilled!'

'And there is still your make-up to do when we get home, and your beautiful new dress. I think—' Ling San put her head on one side '—that your Blake will fall in love with his wife all over again.'

Maggie smiled and said nothing. But a hope was surfacing that tonight Blake might see her as a different person altogether, a charming, soigneé young woman that he would be proud to introduce to any of his friends as his wife. She thought of the pride and tenderness in Dietrich Hauser's face when he looked at Ling San. If ever Blake looked at her like that she would ask nothing more of life. Suddenly, and perhaps unreasonably, she felt exhilarated.

But later on, when the time had come to set out from the Hausers' apartment, the exhilaration had turned to nerves and there was a sick feeling in the pit of her stomach. She wasn't used to dress-up parties; she wasn't used to mixing with the rich, fashionable people that the Hausers would invite. And worst of all, she didn't know how Blake was going to take the 'new' Maggie. If she could have depended on his support she would have felt confident about carrying off her new image, but the fact was, she couldn't.

'Hurry, you two,' Dietrich called from the front door, where his opulent car stood waiting. 'We must not allow the proprietress to arrive late.'

Ling San came into Maggie's room, exquisite in a jade green cheongsam, heavily embroidered round the straight, slashed skirt and the little stand-up collar, her hair gleaming like a blackbird's wing.

'You look lovely, Ling San,' Maggie said warmly.

The Chinese girl smiled composedly. 'Thank you, Maggie, and so do you.'

Maggie had spent quite a proportion of her first month's allowance from Blake on her outfit for tonight, and she and Ling San had spent a whole afternoon choosing it.

Now she took a last look at herself in the mirror and could hardly believe what she saw there. Her dress was of matt satin in a creamy-coffee colour that almost exactly matched her hair. The top was off-the-shoulder, draped sensuously over her breast and embroidered with tiny pearl beads. The skirt was finely pleated and swung round her long, slender legs, glistening dully in the light as she moved. Bronze kid sandals with high heels and a satin clutch bag with a pearl clasp completed the outfit. She wore no jewellery except a gold bracelet that had been a twenty-first present from her parents.

Her skin, under Ling San's expert attention, was creamy and as smooth as the satin of her dress, her lips moist and inviting, her eyes large and luminous.

Ling San regarded her work of art critically, and moved forward to touch her little finger delicately to one corner of Maggie's eye. 'Yes, that shadow is just right. Your eyes have a mysterious glow, like the depths of a forest in autumn.'

Maggie giggled nervously. 'I do love your poetic flights, Ling San. I just hope I can live up to your hopes and bring all the rich women piling into the salon.'

Ling San nodded sagely. 'You will,' she said confidently. 'You have that look that all women want these days.'

'And what kind of look is that?'

The Chinese girl put her head on one side in her mischievous way, 'Sexy,' she said.

When they arrived at the salon Nick Grant was waiting outside the locked door. 'Thought you might use some help with serving the champagne,' he grinned at Dietrich.

Inside, when the lights were switched on and Ling San was setting out plates of bite-size savouries, Nick took Maggie's hands and drew her towards one of the softly-shaded lights. He drew in a breath, blinking as if he were dazzled. 'Well, I'm rocked back on my heels. I always knew you were lovely, Maggie, but this is ridiculous!'

They all laughed and Ling San looked delighted.

Maggie twirled gaily, the finely-pleated satin skirt slapping against her slender legs. 'The new Maggie—all done by magic—and Ling San, of course.'

Ling San and her husband started to set out the snacks and canapés with wine glasses, and Maggie and Nick were left standing together.

'Where's Blake got to?' asked Nick, looking round.

'Oh, he's still working, wouldn't you know? I expect he'll be along later on, when he's finished moving his mountain.' She tried to make a joke of it, but Nick didn't smile. He was looking rather oddly at her, but before he could say anything more the first guests began to arrive, and soon the room was full of laughter and chatter and the clink of glasses, with cigar smoke and the soft thrum of background music drifting on the perfumed air.

Maggie met one after another of Dietrich's colleagues, very smooth, very prosperous. The women were expensively dressed, some (she thought) rather overdressed. Ling San could show them a thing or two if they patronised her. But it was the men who lingered round Maggie, re-filling her glass, plying her with pâté, admiring her with their eyes. She smiled at them and answered their questions lightly, but all the time her glance kept straying towards the doorway.

Nick was circulating with a tray. 'Blake not turned up yet?'

She shook her head. 'Not yet.'

He put down the tray and slipped a hand under her elbow. 'Then I must be stand-in once again. Come along, I want you to meet some friends of mine.'

She turned to go with him, but stopped abruptly, her heart missing a beat, her gaze riveted on the wide arcade outside the entrance to the salon, where tourists were strolling along, pausing to admire the displays.

Nick stared into her face. 'What's up, Maggie? You look as if you've seen a ghost.'

'I'm—I'm all right,' she whispered. 'I just thought——'

It *couldn't* be Fiona Deering, could it, that girl who had just passed by on the far side of the arcade? The same white-gold hair, falling to the shoulders of the shocking-pink silk suit; the same graceful, swaying walk of the trained model, the same insolent tilt of the small rounded chin.

No, it was too much of a coincidence—it couldn't be Fiona. However brutal Blake had been after the wedding, he wouldn't bring Fiona here without telling her. Their relationship had been so much more friendly lately. Surely—*surely* he wouldn't do that to her?

She swallowed. 'I thought I recognised somebody out there,' she told Nick, moving away from the window, 'but I was mistaken. Are those your friends over there? There's somebody waving to you.'

Nick didn't move. He continued to hold Maggie's arm and his pleasant, fair face was very serious. 'Maggie dear,' he said in a low tone, bending his head close to hers to make himself heard above the chatter, 'I wanted to tell you that I'm going back to the U.K. on tonight's flight. I'm almost on my way now.'

'Oh, Nick, are you really?' She felt a quick stab of disappointment. 'I thought you were here for the duration of the job.'

'No,' he said, 'only a stand-in for another fellow. That seems to be my role at present.' He smiled crookedly. 'I really didn't intend coming tonight, but I had to see you to say goodbye. I haven't seen anything of you lately, I thought it was wiser to keep away, but I wanted to reassure myself that all was well now between you and Blake after that—other time.'

'Oh—absolutely,' Maggie said blithely. 'No problems at all.'

'You're *sure*? You're not holding out on me?'

'Nick!' She gave him a baffled smile. 'What *is* this—a marriage guidance council?'

She expected him to grin back and make some apology, but he said doggedly, 'If you need it.'

She stiffened. Nick was a friend, but this was too much interference altogether. 'Thank you very much, but I don't,' she said coolly.

'Good, that was all I wanted to know. But just remember that if you ever need a friend——' He looked hard at her for a moment. 'Goodbye, Maggie,' he said. He walked away from her and was lost in the crowd.

She stood quite still, looking after him. Nick was altogether too perceptive, but this time he was wrong. A little while ago she might have turned to him for help, but now she and Blake were back on their old terms and she didn't need help from anyone, she told herself staunchly. Blake wouldn't let her down. Oh, where was he—why didn't he come?

At that moment, as if her longing had reached him, she saw him turning in through the wide doorway and her heart gave a great thud and started to beat furiously against her ribs. He stood looking around, frowning slightly, and his glance passed over her without stopping. The change was complete—he actually didn't recognise her!

She ran towards him, her brown eyes brilliant with a joy she didn't attempt to hide. Let him believe she was just acting the loving wife if he wanted to. 'Blake—you made it after all!' Her heart swelled with pride. In his immaculately-fitting grey suit and snowy silk shirt he was so much the most handsome, distinguished man in the whole room, so tall and dark and so utterly masculine.

'Maggie!' he gasped. His frown turned to amazement. He took both her hands and held her a little way away. 'It *is* Maggie, is it—this gorgeous woman?'

He was laughing down at her and his grey eyes were soft, as she had dreamed of seeing them. There was tenderness in his face; he was looking at her as a man looks at the girl he loves—just as Dietrich looked at Ling San. Telling her without words that she was the most precious thing in the whole world.

The miracle had happened and Maggie could say

nothing. She couldn't take it in all at once.

He touched the swathed satin at her breast. 'Pretty dress,' he said. 'I like it.'

She gulped. 'I'm glad,' she said stupidly. She felt ridiculously shy. Then she pulled herself together. 'Come and meet everyone, there's lots of champagne flowing.'

She took his hand and began to urge him towards the bar that Dietrich had improvised at the far end of the salon. She was dizzy with happiness, as if she were floating inches above the thick pile carpet.

'Maggie—stop a minute!' He was resisting the pressure of her hand. She turned questioningly. 'Maggie, I——' he looked embarrassed '—I'm terribly sorry, but I'm afraid I can't stay. I just looked in to tell you.' He pulled a rueful face. 'You know how it is. Something's come up and it's extremely important—something that I have to deal with straight away.' She must have looked stricken, for he said again, 'I really am sorry, I wouldn't have missed your party for the world if I could have helped it.' He might have been consoling a child who had been denied a treat.

'Is it—do you *have* to go? Is it all that important?' she wailed.

'Yes.' He looked stern suddenly, unapproachable, the way he looked when you asked him questions at your peril. 'I have to go, and I'm not sure when I'll be back, but you'll be O.K. You're on the hotel premises.' He put a hand briefly on her shoulder. 'Forgive me, Maggie?'

The old Blake spoke there. He always said 'Forgive me, Maggie,' when he had asked her to do something unpleasant or difficult.

She said with a sigh, as she had always said, 'I suppose so.'

'Make my apologies to Ling San and Dietrich,' he

said, 'and I'll see you later on, as soon as I can get away. We must talk, Maggie, there are important things to be discussed.'

He stood very still for a moment, and his eyes moved slowly over her, over the supple satin vest that moulded her youthful figure, to the froth of pleats round her long, slender legs. 'You look very lovely,' he said gently.

He lifted his hand in a little salute and strode away, out into the shopping arcade.

Maggie felt as if the smile were built permanently into her face. She followed him and stood in the open doorway, watching his tall form moving purposefully between the sauntering window-shoppers.

He loved her—she was sure of it. He had told her so in everything but words; the look on his face had been unmistakable. And when he came back—'there are important things to be discussed' he had said. She put a hand to her breast, where he had touched her. *Tonight*, she thought, and joy ran like wine in her blood. Tonight, at last, it was all going to come right.

He was nearly at the end of the arcade now; she could just make out his dark head, towering above all the other heads around him. He stopped and she lifted a hand to wave, expecting him to turn round.

Then her breath caught in her throat and her body went rigid as she stared down the length of the arcade. Blake had been joined by a woman in a shocking-pink suit. Even from this distance the colour stood out plainly, and the long white-gold hair that fell to the collar of her jacket. Their two figures merged together in the passing crowd and from the distance it looked as if she put her arms round his neck and drew his head down to hers. For a moment they stood there, then they moved on together and disappeared round the corner of the arcade.

Maggie gripped the edge of the heavy glass door. She had been right, then—it *was* Fiona Deering who had passed a few minutes ago. Blake had brought her out to Hong Kong because he couldn't live without her. It was painfully clear why he should have been away night after night. He had been with Fiona. The easy friendliness he had shown lately had been a cloak—a trick to keep her, Maggie, happy until he could announce his plans. 'There are important things to be discussed,' he had said. Too true there were, she thought bleakly.

She felt sick and she was shaking all over. She couldn't stay here, she must get away, up to her room. She looked round desperately for Ling San, but the Chinese girl was at the far end of the salon, surrounded by a laughing crowd of guests.

Then she saw Nick, standing beside a pillar a short distance away. He came towards her. 'I'm off to the airport now—I didn't want to butt in when Blake was with you——'

He stopped, staring at her. 'Why, Maggie, what's the matter? You look like death!'

She said the first words that came into her head. 'I wish I *was* dead,' she muttered. She lifted stricken eyes to his. 'Nick, get me out of here, *please*, just take me up to my room and then I'll be O.K.'

Nick was his helpful, undemanding self. He asked no questions, just put a firm arm round her waist and led her to the lift. Outside the door to the suite Maggie fumbled blindly in her bag for her key and handed it to him. He opened the door and pushed her gently into a chair.

He said, 'Now take it easy, and I'll find something to pull you together.'

She raised a hand feebly. 'Just a glass of water, please, Nick.'

She heard him in the kitchen and a minute later he put a glass of iced water into her hand.

She took a gulp. 'Nick, I'm sorry—I——'

He had a hand at her wrist, feeling for her pulse. 'Just relax,' he told her. 'Doctor Nick will prescribe.'

'I'm not ill—really. It was just—a shock. Something I wasn't expecting. You know how it takes you.'

'I do indeed.' He sat down opposite. Her head drooped and he peered upwards to see into her face. 'Want to talk about it, love?'

She shook her head dumbly, closing her eyes. Now that the final blow had fallen it was amazing how clear her mind was. The pain was there, lurking in the background, but at this moment she felt nothing but an urgent need to get away. The end had come between her and Blake. There had been too much deceit, too much betrayal on both their parts, for any relationship to be patched up again between them. She must leave here as soon as possible.

And above all else Blake mustn't know that she was pregnant. At best he might think that she was using the baby as a bargaining point—to make him stay with her. At worst he might try to persuade her to have an abortion, which she wouldn't agree to under any circumstances. If she couldn't have the man she loved, she could at least have his child.

She lifted her head and looked into Nick's kind, worried face. 'Nick—you said you would help me if I ever needed help.'

He nodded soberly. 'And I meant every word of it.'

'Well, I need it now—desperately. Will you help me to get out of Hong Kong and fly back to England? Will you do this without asking for any explanations or reasons?'

There was the shortest of pauses. She saw the sympathy in Nick's face. And there was hope, too. He had guessed from the moment they met at Macau that all wasn't well between her and Blake. 'Anything you say, Maggie,' he said simply. 'And no strings attached. When do you want to go?'

She laughed shakily. 'Now, this minute. Sooner if possible.' It wasn't possible, of course, and somehow she would have to avoid having any sort of a showdown with Blake.

Nick said thoughtfully, 'It might be managed—if you're really desperate, Maggie. Could you be ready to leave in—' he looked at his watch '—in about ten minutes? I've got a taxi ordered to take me to the airport. When we're there we could see if something could be fixed up. If there's no seat available on this flight—and I shouldn't think there will be—perhaps it could be arranged for you to take my ticket and I would travel on a later flight. I'm not in any great hurry.'

'Oh, Nick, if only you could——' She broke off, biting her lip. 'I'm taking advantage of your good nature and I shouldn't——'

He said drily, 'I can recognise an urgent need to escape when I see it, girl. Come along, get into some travelling clothes, pack a bag and let's get out of here.'

He didn't add, '—before Blake gets back,' but she knew that was what he was thinking.

In the end, Maggie travelled alone. She stood beside Nick outside Passport Control and wished he were coming with her. 'Thank you, Nick, you've been wonderful. I can't tell you—Oh goodness——' a hand flew to her mouth—'I should have left a note or something for Blake.' She tried to smile as she added, 'All runaway wives leave a note, don't they?' but the smile was a ghastly failure. She was remembering that other note she had written the night before her wedding. The one she had torn up.

Nick pulled out notebook and pencil. 'Scribble something,' he said, 'I'll see Blake gets it.' His face was deadpan. He wasn't saying what he thought of Blake, but he was making his opinion quite obvious: if Maggie had found her marriage unbearable, then the fault wasn't on her side.

She took the pencil and wrote: 'I can't take any more, Blake. I need to get away by myself. I'll contact you when I feel able to, and we can make arrangements about a divorce.' She started to write 'Sorry about——' and then crossed it out. There were faults on both sides, but she didn't think she need apologise to Blake for anything.

She gave the notebook back to Nick and he tore out the page, folded it and put it in an inside pocket. 'No other message?'

'No,' she said. 'Goodbye, Nick, and thanks again for everything.' She reached up and kissed him quickly and gratefully.

'I'll see you?' He made it into a question.

She knew what he was asking. 'Give me time, Nick dear,' she said.

'Of course. Well, you know where to find me. It's up to you, Maggie.'

She nodded and picked up her hand luggage. Nick stood looking after her, a twisted little smile on his mouth, until she disappeared among the passengers, but despite her gratitude Maggie had forgotten him almost immediately. For now, after all this time, despair had taken over completely. She was leaving Blake behind—

soon he would be half a world away from her—and if she ever saw him again it would be to arrange a divorce. The tears gathered thickly in her eyes as she stood in the queue at the passport control desk, waiting her turn. She had been so sure, at the salon, so wonderfully, joyously sure, that the tenderness in his eyes, in his voice, had meant that he loved her.

But she had been mistaken. It had not been love, it had merely been pity.

CHAPTER EIGHT

'AND that's how it was,' Maggie told Catriona, some forty-eight hours later. 'When I got to London I booked in at a hotel, but I couldn't settle down on my own. I was trying to pluck up courage to go home and face Mother, but in the end I funked it and—so I got on another plane and came up here to you.' She glanced apologetically at her sister-in-law. 'I'm afraid I've rather barged in on you, Catriona, I hope you don't mind too much.'

She shivered. She had been shivering on and off since she got on to the plane at Hong Kong. Her sister-in-law said briskly, 'You're cold, Maggie.' She got up and threw a couple more logs on the fire in the huge hearth. 'That's the worst of living in the North—the summer's soon over.' She went across the big, comfortable room and pulled the curtains, shutting out the darkening, tree-fringed garden. Then she sat down again and studied Maggie's slender form, hunched up in the corner of the sofa.

'I'm very glad you did come to me, Maggie dear, but I'm sorry things have turned out like this so soon. Are you quite sure Blake wants this other woman?'

Maggie nodded. 'Quite sure. She was his old love and she turned up again. It's happened before. Just a sordid little eternal triangle, and I didn't fancy being the odd one out.' She winced, remembering the two of them meeting and kissing in that shopping arcade.

Catriona's eyes were warmly affectionate. 'You must stay with us as long as you want—until the bairn comes, if that suits you. I'd like fine to have a bairn in the house again.'

Tears gathered thickly in Maggie's eyes. It was embarrassing not to know, from one moment to the next, when she would start to cry helplessly. On the plane from Hong Kong she had worn dark glasses, but the stewardess had spotted that she was upset and had been kind and concerned and tempted her with a special cocktail. Everyone had been so kind—Nick, Catriona, even the stewardess whose name she didn't know. Everyone but the one person whose kindness she wanted most. And *he* didn't care about her at all. She fumbled for a handkerchief and blew her nose, feeling a moment's anger with herself. It was so out of character for her to go to bits like this. 'I'm just being silly,' she gulped. 'Sorry, Catriona.'

Catriona moved to the sofa beside her and patted her arm. 'You've had a bad time, my dear, and what you need now is rest. A nice warm bed and a good sleep. Come along now, I've put the electric blanket on, and your room's warm.'

As they climbed the stairs Maggie whispered, 'James? What's he going to think?'

'Och, don't you worry your head about James. Your

brother's very, very fond of you; he'll back you up any way he can. And the girls will be thrilled to have you here. Jessie's old enough to understand that you've come back to have your baby because the climate in Hong Kong is too hot. That's the way we'll put it to them when James brings them home from their party in Edinburgh shortly. I won't let them disturb you tonight, you need your sleep.'

Maggie looked at the cosy bed, its white coverlet shading pink in the glow from the electric fire, and doubted whether she would ever sleep again. Her head felt as if it were full of buzzing insects, skittering round and round, but she thanked her sister-in-law and dutifully slid out of her clothes and into the warm bed.

'That's fine now.' Catriona appeared again with a glass of malted milk and a plate of buttered oatcakes. She indicated two white tablets on the tray. 'Swallow these, they're quite harmless,' she said, 'and I'll guarantee you'll sleep the clock round. Goodnight, Maggie dear.' She leaned and kissed Maggie's cheek, a rare gesture from the unemotional Catriona.

Alone in the room, Maggie sipped the malted milk, forced a bite or two of the oatcakes down her dry throat, and pushed the tablets out of their plastic moulds.

'Sleep the clock round,' Catriona had said. Maggie swallowed the tablets, turned out the light and closed her eyes. She wouldn't much care if she never wakened again.

For five days she lived from hour to hour, from minute to minute, refusing to allow herself to think of the future. She was almost sure now about the baby, and Catriona persuaded her to visit her own doctor, who confirmed what she had suspected.

The doctor was an elderly Scot, grey-haired, with shrewd eyes and a kindly smile. He looked keenly at Maggie's white, strained face and said, 'Your sister-in-law tells me you've been living in Hong Kong?'

'Yes, I—I found the climate too much for me this time of the year. Terribly hot and humid, and there was always the risk of typhoons. I—persuaded—my husband to let me come back to Britain for a time.'

The doctor's eyes narrowed. 'And your husband? He's staying out there?'

'Oh yes, he has to. His work——' She couldn't meet the doctor's searching gaze.

He nodded thoughtfully. 'I see. Well, your sister-in-law will look after you fine. A practical, sensible body!'

Maggie left the surgery with a wad of leaflets and an appointment at the ante-natal clinic.

She visited the clinic next day and tried not to notice the curious glances of the other young mothers-to-be. She knew she looked ill—her mirror told her so—and one or two of the others tried to draw her sympathetically into their circle, but Maggie found herself quite unable to join in the friendly exchange of progress reports and knitting patterns, so after a time they left her alone.

The days passed with a strange, oppressive sense of unreality. Her brother James was all for telephoning out to Blake and challenging him to 'put his cards on the table' as he expressed it, but Maggie persuaded him to do nothing for the present and he grumblingly agreed. Catriona was her own kindly, practical self and was obviously trying to make Maggie's life seem as ordinary and calm as was possible in the circumstances.

Jessie and Jean were the greatest comfort. They were on holiday from school and rapturous that Auntie Maggie had suddenly appeared in their midst. They were

avidly interested in the coming baby and fussed round
Maggie like two little old women, bringing her a foot-
stool and making her put her feet up, enquiring solici-
tously whether she was feeling tired, tempting her with
snacks filched from the kitchen when their mother
wasn't looking. 'Because you have to eat for two, now,
Auntie Maggie,' Jessie assured her solemnly.

Catriona remonstrated with them not to bother their
aunt, but Maggie pleaded, 'Oh, do let them stay. They're
such darlings and they help me to——'

To what? To forget? But there was no hope of doing
that. The memories were too vivid and too painful.

She wrote to Ling San, saying how truly sorry she
was to have had to leave at such short notice, without
saying goodbye or explaining. 'But I could see that the
opening ceremony was going splendidly and I'm sure
you will be really successful with the new venture. Nick
may have explained a little about my difficulties. I only
hope that one day we may meet again and meanwhile,
the very best of luck with "Nu Yu".'

From day to day she put off contacting her parents in
Amersham. It would have to be done soon, but the
prospect appalled her. Catriona was a little perturbed
that Maggie's mother should be left in the dark. 'Would
you like me to ring her and explain a little?' she suggested. 'I'd be tactful and not alarm her.'

Maggie went very white. 'Oh, just give me one more
day. There's so much she doesn't know and it's going to
upset her dreadfully. She was so happy about my marriage and she never dreamed that everything wasn't
right.' She paused. 'But *you* did, didn't you, Catriona?'

Her sister-in-law looked wry. 'It was only a sixth
sense,' she said apologetically. 'I just felt that one day
you might need a refuge—we all do sometimes. But you

will let them know tomorrow, won't you, Maggie? Promise me.'

Maggie nodded. 'I'll ring home tomorrow evening, when Daddy's back,' she said.

After lunch next day Catriona said, 'I've got a dental appointment this afternoon and I'll be gone a while. Mr Stewart's mother is more or less confined to the house with arthritis and I always look in to have a chat with her when I'm there. Do you mind being left on your own, Maggie? James is coming home early to take the girls to the swimming baths. It's a weekly ritual and he looks forward to it.' She hesitated. 'Would you like to go along too?'

Maggie shook her head. 'No, I won't go with them, I think,' she said, and she thought Catriona looked slightly relieved. Probably James liked to have his daughters to himself now and again. 'I'll be okay. It's a gorgeous day—I'll go for a walk in the glen and get back in time to have tea ready for the swimmers. I'll make some of those gingerbread biscuits the girls like, shall I?'

James's home lay some miles from Edinburgh, in a fold of the hills. The long garden ended in a wild patch, known to the family as 'the wilderness'. Beyond that a stile opened the way to a little glen. Protected from the winds by the hills around, low-growing trees flourished and a tiny stream bubbled down from the hill above. The girls loved 'their' glen and Maggie had spent hours playing with them here in the few days she had been in Scotland. Walking alone here now she tried to keep remembering the fun the girls had had, and close her mind to her constant yearning for Blake. It was weak and absurd, this continuing passion for him when he didn't want her and had shown her so in no uncertain way. Where was her pride? she asked herself. Why couldn't she hate him?

She walked along slowly, the turf soft under her feet, the dead leaves crackling as she walked. It had taken longer than she expected to make the ginger biscuits and it was almost time to turn back, to be there when James and the girls arrived home, tired and hungry as they certainly would be.

She paused, watching the stream bubbling over its stones, incredibly clear and pure. The mist was getting up now, rising from the ground like puffs of white smoke and the autumn air had turned chilly without warning, as it did in the North.

She shivered. The little glen seemed to have lost its charm suddenly, to have become a cold, forbidding place. She turned and began to run through the rising mist—straight into the arms of a man who had approached silently from the direction of the house.

Maggie gave a little gasp. 'Oh, I'm sorry, James, I didn't see——' She blinked up at him. 'Blake! Wh-what are you doing here?'

He stood impassively, holding on to her arms, where he had caught her in her flight. 'I'd have thought it obvious. Looking for my wife, of course.'

She thought she was going to faint. She must be dreaming—or going mad. In the semi-gloom she thought she saw that tenderness in his face again. But she wasn't going to be taken in this time.

She drew away from him. 'You didn't need to come all this way, surely? I promised to get in touch. I would have done in a day or two. I—I just wanted to be alone for a bit. To think things out.'

'What is there to think out?' he enquired.

'Oh, Blake—surely——' Her voice trembled un-

controllably. 'You don't have to pretend to be so dim.
You and I, of course, and our marriage. And Fiona.'

'Ah!' he breathed. 'I think I see now. You saw Fiona
in Hong Kong and you jumped to certain conclusions?'

She began to walk quickly towards the house and he
fell into step beside her. Suddenly she stopped and faced
him. 'How did you know I was here?' she asked.

'I didn't, but it wasn't too difficult to discover.
Naturally I thought you'd make for your home in
Amersham. But I didn't want to waste time going there,
so I contacted your father at his office.'

She gasped. 'You've got a nerve, Blake! I didn't want
to upset my parents—that's why I came here. My
mother and father don't know—anything.'

'So I gathered,' he said dryly. 'I had a bit of explaining
to do, but in the end I managed to convince your father
that there'd been a stupid misunderstanding and ask his
advice as to where I might find you. This was the first
place he thought of. He phoned through to your sister-
in-law this morning. I had a word with her myself and
she suggested I come straight up here and talk to you.'

'She had no right to,' she said, her voice shaking. 'I
didn't want to see you again.'

'Didn't you? Didn't you, Maggie? Are you telling me
the truth?'

'Yes,' she said defiantly. She tried to draw further
away from him, but the path between the trees was
narrow, and she was uncomfortably conscious of the
tall, hard body so close to her own as he adjusted his
pace to stay beside her. She quickened her steps, stumbling over buried tree roots. She had to get away before
that fatal chemistry began to work in her blood. Already
she felt weak with longing to throw herself into his arms,
to plead for—for what? A new beginning for them? How

futile could you get?

'Well, that's a pity,' he said, 'because I wanted to see you. I've come half-way round the world to do it, as you may have noticed.' His voice was tense; she recognised that he was holding himself under control with difficulty.

'Oh, I have noticed. I think you've wasted your time. I'm perfectly willing to agree to a divorce on any terms you like, if that's what you wanted to ask me.'

'It wasn't what I wanted to ask you,' he said grimly.

Suddenly he gripped her arm and spun her round to face him. She struggled, but he had hold of her other arm now and she was helpless.

'I'm tired of pussyfooting around like this—you've got to listen to me, Maggie.' He shook her, not very gently, and she heard the familiar anger rising in his voice.

'I don't want to hear—let me go!'

'Shut up!' He gave her another shake.

She was almost in tears now. 'Why can't you leave me alone, Blake? I told you I'd agree to a divorce, if you're so desperate to marry Fiona.'

He lifted his head to the overhanging branches. 'Oh God, what a stubborn little chump it is! Now listen, you——' He gave her another shake and her teeth chattered. 'I *don't* want to marry Fiona. I can't think of anything I'd like less than to be married to Fiona. And I can't think of anything I'd like more than to be married to you, Maggie. And I mean married. Not this stupid game we've been playing for weeks. I know I behaved badly, but that was some time ago and since then things have changed.'

She stared at him blankly as the mist swirled round him, blurring his expression, glistening on his face, on his dark hair. His eyes were colourless, holding hers like steel magnets. She couldn't look away.

'Just—just put it into plain words, will you?' she said shakily.

There was a short silence and she heard his quick intake of breath. 'I love you,' he said. 'I can't put it plainer that that. And I think maybe I could make you love me, given time.'

Maggie was silent. These were the words she had longed to hear from him, dreamed of hearing, but now she had heard them there was a blank feeling of un- reality, of anti-climax. He didn't really love her, he couldn't. Not all of a sudden like this. He was once again using her for some plan of his own.

She said in a small voice, 'Thank you for telling me, Blake. Now, I think we should go in, the others will have come home by now.'

'No,' he rapped out. 'Give me a chance, for God's sake!' His arm shot out with a violence that shocked her. His mouth came down on hers and it was hard and angry, and cold with the wet mist that covered both their faces. His lips moved savagely on hers as if he could somehow force a response from her. For a moment she submitted, then her whole body stiffened with resistance. She couldn't—*wouldn't*—go through all that again. The burning desire, the promise of heaven, the bitter disappointment.

Summoning all her strength, she wrenched herself away from him and ran towards the house. He caught her up as she was pushing open the side door into the hall and she turned to confront him. 'Go away, Blake, I don't want you here,' she hissed.

She didn't know how he would have replied, for at that moment Catriona opened the door from the inside, smiling at them both, but, it seemed, particularly at Blake.

'You found her, then?' She shook his hand. 'Welcome to Edinburgh, Blake. You know it, I expect?'

She was playing the hostess, ignoring any emotional undertones, taking care not to meet Maggie's accusing eyes.

Blake took his cue and followed Catriona as she led the way into the drawing-room, where James was dispensing drinks. James had evidently been primed by his wife, for he, too, greeted Blake amiably and put a drink in his hand, enquiring about his journey. Nobody seemed to notice Maggie's silence.

'What'll you have, Sis?' her brother asked. 'This is something of an occasion, we must celebrate.'

The situation was getting more and more false by the moment. Maggie felt she was on the verge of bursting into hysterical laughter, and a drink might help. 'Gin and lemon, please,' she said, and swallowed it down quickly.

'Jessie and Jean are having their tea in the kitchen,' Catriona said. 'Wolfing down your ginger biscuits, Maggie. Swimming always gives them a terrific appetite.'

'I'll go and see them,' said Maggie, seizing on any opportunity to get out of range of those magnetic grey-green eyes that she could feel on her, even though she didn't see them.

'Yes, do,' Catriona smiled. 'You go along with her, Blake, the girls would love to see you. James and I have to attend to our livestock and close up the greenhouses.' Catriona kept chickens and grew all her own vegetables. 'It's going to be a chilly night. Come along, Jimmy.'

James followed her out of the room. Blake met Maggie's eyes and smiled ironically. 'Too bad!' he drawled. 'You can't get away from me, can you?'

Maggie said as nastily as she knew how, 'You read me like a book.'

'I wish I could,' he said, following her into the kitchen.

The girls screeched with pleasure as Maggie went in, and became suddenly shy and silent as Blake appeared behind her.

'Hullo, you two,' he greeted them amiably. 'Enjoying the ginger biscuits? Got one to spare for a weary traveller?'

Jessie stood up and offered the plate of biscuits politely. 'Do have one,' she said, in her best grown-up manner, 'I'm sure you'll like them.'

'I'm sure I will, if Auntie Maggie baked them.' He perched on the free end of the big table, swinging one leg and looking very much at home. 'And what have you been doing at the swimming baths? Breaststroke, butterfly, crawl?'

'Daddy says I crawl like a—a cattypillar,' giggled Jean. Both the girls lost their shyness at that, and Blake was given an excited account of the various accomplishments of the session, both girls talking at once. He listened with every sign of interest. Quite one of the family! Maggie thought, barely able to control a desire to run out of the kitchen. Instead, she went across to the sink and busied herself washing up the cooking utensils she had used, and had already washed once.

Blake went on acting the jolly, affectionate uncle to Jessie and Jean and they went on lapping it up until Maggie cold have screamed, 'Don't listen to him, he doesn't mean a word of it.' She wished she knew why he was taking such pains to be charming to her family. Certainly he hadn't done so before. Before the wedding he hadn't bothered to visit her home, except one duty visit, and certainly hadn't put himself out to ingratiate himself with her parents.

And now, after all that had happened, he suddenly appeared and professed to love her, made himself charming to her family, and showed every sign of wanting to keep her with him. It didn't make sense.

Her mind was so busy with the problem that she didn't at first take in what Jean had just said. Then, in the abrupt silence that followed, the words formed themselves into a sentence, with awful clarity.

'Have you come to take Auntie Maggie away?' Jean had piped, and Maggie could still hear the childish voice echoing through the kitchen. ''Cos we don't want her to go. We want her to stay here and have her baby.'

CHAPTER NINE

THE silence continued, spreading out like a pool. Even Jessie didn't seem to have anything to say. Maggie couldn't look at Blake, she went on polishing the baking tray furiously, with her back to him.

He came slowly across the room and put both hands on her shoulders. 'Well, Maggie,' he said, '*are* you coming back to Hong Kong with me to have your baby?'

He turned her round to face him and she met his eyes. There was laughter lurking in them. 'This is absolutely ridiculous,' she said weakly.

'I agree,' he said solemnly. 'Suppose we go somewhere to discuss the matter in private?' He turned to the two little girls. 'We'll let you know later,' he said. He put an arm round Maggie and propelled her out of the kitchen and up the stairs.

They halted on the landing. 'Which is our room?' he asked blandly.

'*My* room,' she corrected. 'I haven't invited you to stay.' She had herself under control now. Of course, Blake would have to know about the baby; it was just unfortunate that he should have taken Jean's remark as a joke. It would make it all the harder to tell him, and she had a horrid fear that he would be angry.

He followed her in and closed the door. Then he stood looking round the big, airy room. 'Nice bedroom,' he said. 'We should be very comfortable here for a day or two. Catriona has invited me to stay until the weekend. Monday was the earliest I could book a return flight to Hong Kong for both of us on the same flight. I thought we could travel down on Saturday and look in on your parents before we leave.'

Maggie sank down into a chair by the window. 'Aren't you taking a lot for granted?'

'It's the only way with you, my girl. If I don't keep my eye on you you're liable to do all sorts of crazy things.' He came and stood behind her chair. 'Like having your hair cut in this chic style. I like it.' He ran his fingers through her short hair and at his touch a thrill ran through her right down to her toes, but she sat rigid, her back to him, staring out of the window into the darkness outside. 'You knocked me for six when I saw you at Ling San's party,' he went on. 'I always knew you could look gorgeous if you wanted to. But you never bothered before, did you? You were always so busy giving the impression of a capable young woman engineer.'

She looked up then, startled. 'Is that how you saw me? A girl trying to prove myself in a man's world?'

'Sometimes,' he said, smiling. 'And sometimes I saw you in the way a man usually sees an attractive woman. And you probably know how that is.'

She flushed deeply. 'I—I didn't think you saw me at all,' she said, 'except as a good colleague.'

'Oh yes,' he moved his fingers from her hair and slid them down her neck to her shoulders and over her soft, swelling breasts. 'Lots of times I looked at you and wondered what you'd say if I made—er—certain improper suggestions. But you never gave me the slightest encouragement, and I just didn't know. I didn't want to risk spoiling our working relationship, so I suppose I went on taking the easy ladies. But they never amounted to much.'

'Until Fiona?'

He moved away and sat down on the dressing table stool, close to her.

'Yes, until Fiona. I suppose a man is allowed one crazy adolescent infatuation in his life. She played hard to get at first, and that was a challenge. Oh yes, for a few insane weeks I heard the siren song all right.'

'A few *weeks*? Oh no, it lasted longer than that—you brought her out to Hong Kong. You left the party at Ling San's to be with her. You never told me what you were doing. That was why I left—I couldn't take any more. I saw you together—kissing.'

Blake glared at her. 'You saw nothing of the sort. I was trying against my better judgment, to get Fiona out of an unholy mess she'd got into. You may have seen her expressing her gratitude, but that was all. I couldn't wait to get the business finished and get back to you, Maggie. I wanted to talk to you, to break through the wall that we'd put up between us. I wanted to make love to you again. God, how I wanted to!'

He leaned forward and put his hands at her waist, urging her out of her chair towards him. She looked at his eyes, his mouth, and suddenly she relaxed. All her resistance went and a warm tide of longing ran through her. She let herself be drawn towards him, held against him, and she could feel him begin to tremble as their bodies touched in intimate contact.

He put up his hands and smoothed back her hair. 'Maggie?' he questioned huskily, and she lowered her mouth to receive his kiss.

She kissed him back hungrily. This didn't make sense, but it didn't matter. Blake was here and she was in his arms now, and he was carrying her towards the bed, pulling her clothes off with deft urgent hands. Her arms seemed to move of their own accord, going up round his neck as his mouth claimed hers again in a long kiss, then moved downward to caress her throat, her breast, while his hands set off little explosions along her nerves. This time there was no brutality in his lovemaking. His hands moved slowly, touching her with experienced fingers, rousing new, overwhelming sensations in her body; giving as well as getting, the ultimate pleasure. Maggie's surrender was complete and asked no questions. It was enough that this was happening to them, that they should be sharing this joy.

'My little love,' he groaned close to her ear. 'My darling——' and she cried out in an ecstasy of fulfilment.

Later they lay quiet together in the darkened room. Maggie was the first to regain her senses. She stirred in Blake's arms and murmured, 'What will Catriona think?'

He rolled towards her and rubbed his rough cheek against hers. 'I'd say she would be making an informed guess as to what we're doing. But if you like I'll go down and check.'

She giggled. 'It might be polite, as guests, to find out what time she wants us to appear for supper.'

Lying back lazily, she watched him while he dressed,

revelling in the strength and suppleness of his tall body, in the way his muscles rippled beneath the thin stuff of his shirt. He picked up her comb from the dressing-table and raked it through his dark hair. 'Am I fit to be seen?'

'You look wonderful,' she sighed, and he came over and kissed her behind her ear and whispered, 'That's what I like to hear.'

He made for the door. 'What shall I tell Jean about the baby? She's a priceless kid, isn't she? They do so love to make up fairy stories. I imagine babies figure strongly in hers.'

Maggie put her hands behind her head on the pillow. 'But it wasn't a fairy story, you know.'

Blake was arrested half-way to the door. He spun round. '*What*?'

'There is a baby,' she said. 'Or will be in about seven and a half months.'

'You mean——' He came back slowly and sat on the bed, staring at her in silence until belief dawned. 'But— oh lord, we shouldn't have——' he gestured towards the tumbled bed. 'Should we?'

'I don't know,' said Maggie happily. 'But we can't undo what we did, thank goodness.'

Very gently he stretched out and touched her cheek. 'Gosh!' he exclaimed, and he sounded like a boy again. 'It's amazing and wonderful. You're glad?'

'If you are,' she said, and saw the answer in his face. She gave him a little push. 'Now, go along and enquire about supper,' and he went, a dazed look on his face.

When he had gone Maggie got up and showered and put on the prettiest of the two dresses she had brought with her. She had only had time to cram a few things into her hand-satchel, and fortunately she had hit upon one that she liked particularly. It was a very fine wool, in a dark honey colour, with long, fitting sleeves, a moulded bodice, and a box-pleated skirt that opened out when she walked. She brushed her hair into its new style, admiring once again the clever way that Ling San had cut it so that it fell naturally into soft waves that clung to her head and round her ears.

She put on a light make-up; nothing more was needed—the eyes that looked back at her in the mirror were brilliant, the cheeks delicately pink. She had never seen herself look so—so sparkling and radiant. But then she had never been told before that the man she loved loved her. She was bubbling over with joy; she wanted to sing and dance and shout her happiness from the roof-tops so all the world would know.

Blake came back into the room. He stood for a moment with his back to the door, gazing at her as she sat at the dressing-table. 'You look wonderful, Maggie,' he said unevenly. 'I'd like to——' He came across and stood behind her, meeting her eyes in the mirror, his hands slipping over her shoulders to mould themselves round her breasts. 'But I suppose we must be careful now. I shall look after you very well, my darling.' Soberly he added, 'Try to make up for all those bad old times.'

She covered his hands with hers and turned her head up to him, inviting his kiss. It was a very gentle kiss, a butterfly brushing against her mouth, her temples, her closed eyelids. She couldn't have imagined such tenderness in the tough, arrogant Blake. But it left her weak and trembling and wanting more.

She got to her feet. 'We'd better go down,' she said. 'Before——' She left the rest unsaid and he sighed ruefully.

'I suppose so. Catriona says supper in about fifteen minutes. The girls are in bed and would like you to go and say goodnight to them.'

Jessie and Jean were sitting up expectantly in their two small beds. In their flowery pyjamas, with their dark hair falling to their shoulders and their cheeks petal soft, they looked good enough to eat, Maggie thought as she kissed them both and hugged them tightly.

Jean said perkily, 'Isn't Uncle Blake going to kiss us too?'

He laughed delightedly. 'I never refuse an invitation from a lovely lady.' He suited the action to the word and Jean hung round his neck, her shyness forgotten.

'I like you,' she announced shamelessly. 'You're my favrit man from now on.'

'Jean!' her sister remonstrated severely. 'You mustn' say things like that, it's rude.' She looked at Blake, her small face serious. 'Is Auntie Maggie going away with you?' she enquired, biting her lower lip.

Blake nodded soberly. 'I'm afraid so, poppet. But we'll bring the baby to see you as soon as we can.'

Jessie swallowed and smiled bravely. 'Mind you do,' she said in a fair imitation of her mother's voice.

Outside the bedroom Maggie smiled ruefully. 'Poor darling, she was so looking forward to being a little mother to him—her——' She nestled her head against Blake's shoulder. 'What do you want, a girl or a boy?'

He bent and kissed the tip of her nose. 'Twins,' he grinned. 'One of each. Or is that being too greedy?'

They were still laughing when they walked into the dining-room together, arms entwined.

Supper was something of a celebration meal. If James and Catriona had had any doubts about the happy resolution of Maggie's worries they were obviously satisfied that now all was well. James opened a bottle of the vintage wine he kept in the cellar for special occasions and Catriona produced one of her superb steak and kidney puddings.

'Here's to you both,' James raised his glass, and added with a twinkle, 'All three of you,' and Maggie blushed and smiled up at Blake. He smiled into her eyes and kissed her and she felt as if the stars out in the sky had come right down into the room.

'I'm so glad, love,' Catriona said warmly as Maggie followed her into the kitchen when the meal was over. 'I was really getting a bit bothered about you, and when Blake rang up this morning from London and explained that it was all a big mistake it seemed like the answer to a prayer.

Maggie nodded. 'It was stupid of me to run away like that, I see it now.'

Her sister-in-law picked up the coffee tray. 'Don't blame yourself. We all do foolish things sometimes, especially at the beginning of a marriage. We're particularly touchy just then.' She smiled. 'Too often we fash ourselves into quite a state when five minutes' straight talking would clear it all up.'

Maggie remembered those words later, when she was lying curled up in Blake's arms in the big bed upstairs. The curtains were drawn back and the moonlight was throwing mysterious shadows over the room. Blake's head was black against the whiteness of the pillow. Maggie reached up and tangled her fingers in his hair. 'Blake——?'

He moved sleepily and gathered her closer. 'Um?'

'Darling, I know you're dying to sleep off your jet-lag, but before you do there's something I want to know before I can go to sleep too.'

He yawned hugely. 'If you must——' he said.

'I must,' she told him firmly. 'Catriona and Maggie may be convinced by your story, and you may have convinced my father. But there's quite a lot you forgot to tell me, isn't there?'

He groaned. 'Wouldn't it do in the morning?'

'No,' said Maggie. 'This is one time you don't wind me round your little finger. You left me in Macao on what was supposed to be our honeymoon, and went back to England, to another woman. You were crazy to get rid of me and marry her. Now, suddenly, you tell me you're in love with me.'

'So I am,' he murmured. 'Shall I show you?'

'No.' She pulled herself out of his arms and wriggled over to the far edge of the bed. 'I want to know, Blake.'

He raised himself, thrusting a hand through his rumpled hair. His face looked white and drawn in the moonlight and it was all Maggie could do to stop herself putting her arms round him and telling him it didn't matter.

But it did matter, and she would never have any peace until she knew the score. 'I must know why you suddenly changed your mind,' she said.

'Wretched female,' he grumbled. 'Won't let a fellow get his sleep. Is there any coffee left in that flask?'

She poured him some of the coffee that Catriona had thoughtfully left in their room. Blake took a deep swig of it and said, 'That's better. Now—you want a rundown of my movements from the time I left Macao— and left you with Nick Grant.' He stopped abruptly. 'God, if I'd known the risk I was running, leaving you with Nick!'

'Nick was a good friend,' said Maggie staunchly. 'I was so miserable I'd probably have thrown myself in the South China Sea if it hadn't been for him.'

'Were you, Maggie? Were you really miserable because I'd left? I didn't know that either. There was a hell of a lot I didn't know.'

Maggie waited, saying nothing.

'It's not a very pretty story,' Blake went on. 'I got back to my apartment in London late at night. I'd left Fiona there after our wedding—she said she had nowhere to go, so I gave her my keys and told her to use the place as her own.' He laughed bitterly. 'She took that literally. When I let myself in she was—entertaining a man in my bedroom. In point of fact, in my bed. They were having a high old time—they never even realised that I'd come in and seen them. So——' in the moonlight she saw his mouth twist '——I went out again and left them to it. The next morning I saw J.M. at the office and we had a heart-to-heart. I thought the time had come to make a clean breast of it, and I did.' He leaned back and looked up at the ceiling in silence for a while. Then he went on, 'He was surprisingly understanding, on the whole. I think we came closer together in that interview than we've ever been since I was a kid.'

'He's devoted to you, Blake,' Maggie said softly. 'And very proud of you. He's told me so.'

'He told you something else, too, didn't he?' Blake said unexpectedly.

'What do you mean?'

'He told you about Fiona being mixed up in some scandal in Hong Kong, and that if I had married her I should have been turned down for this job I'm doing out there.'

'Yes, he told me that,' Maggie said.

'And that explained why you turned up at the church that day, when I wasn't expecting you to. It was out of loyalty to the company and to J.M. and ——' he added wryly '——perhaps you had some idea of saving me from making a bloody fool of myself, had you?'

Maggie shook her head. 'No, Blake, that didn't enter my mind, honestly. There was—quite a different reason.'

'Such as——?' But she went on shaking her head and wouldn't tell him.

Instead she said, 'You're not going to tell me you suddenly found you were in love with me, after your talk with J.M., are you?'

He laughed hollowly. 'Not suddenly. It grew on me slowly, like a glorious sunrise. I found myself missing you like hell all the time. Missing the way we could talk together, laugh together, missing always knowing you were *there*. I think I must have loved you all these years, my darling, without really knowing it. Do you believe me?' He held out a hand across the bed and Maggie put her own into it and was drawn close to him again.

'I couldn't wait to get back to you, to try and explain, and make it up to you for the way I'd treated you. And I found myself wanting you. Maggie, wanting to hold you in my arms, all the sweetness and the saneness of you. My God, I'd come to my senses all right! Then, the next day, I got that call from Denby, in Hong Kong, retailing the gossip about what was going on between you and Nick Grant, and I think I was out of my mind for a time. I'd never known what jealousy was before, but by God, I knew then. When I got back and sat in our room waiting for you and then you walked in with Nick, that night, I think all the devils in hell got hold of me. I thought I'd lost you, and it was all my own damned fault.'

There was a long silence. He held her gently and stroked her hair. 'Even now I can hardly believe you've forgiven me. You have, haven't you?' he added anxiously.

'Go on,' she said.

'Well, after that I tried to go slowly, to get back on our old terms, and I think it was partly successful. We seemed to be friends again. I didn't dare hurry you, or tell you how I felt.'

She said slowly, 'I knew you'd been out all night, for several nights running. And then I saw you with Fiona, the night of Ling San's party, and I thought—well, it seemed obvious——'

'So you upped and went.' He held her a little closer as if to make sure that she wasn't going to get away again.

She said, 'I had to—because I knew by then about the baby. I thought——' she bit her lip '—I thought you might want me to get rid of it.'

He groaned. 'Oh lord, was I really such a swine to you that you could believe that?' He cradled her in his arms as if he could somehow undo all the harm he had done. 'But you really did get all the wrong ideas, my darling. I hadn't the faintest idea that Fiona was coming out to Hong Kong, needless to say. Apparently the man she had in London had disappeared and she thought she'd have another try at getting me. She borrowed some money from one of her late husband's racing friends to pay for her flight and when she was there she contacted one of the men she knew before. Stupid, of course, but she had implicit faith in her own attractions and she thought she could get him to pay her hotel bills while she came to some arrangement with me. Unfortunately, the man was just on the verge of being picked up by the I.C.A.C. That's the Independent Commission Against Corruption, if you don't know. Fiona was with him at the time and she was picked up too. She panicked and gave them my name and they contacted me. I had to do what I could to get the idiotic girl off the hook. The night of Ling San's party was the time she was to be interrogated and I promised to go along with her. That was when you saw us together, Maggie.'

'I see,' Maggie said slowly. 'And did you? Get her off the hook, I mean?'

'Yes, fortunately, after a long hassle, they believed what I told them, that she'd come out to visit me and knew nothing of her pal's undercover activities. I gave her her fare back home and told her to keep out of my life in future, or else——'

There was a long silence when he finished speaking. They lay together, their arms round each other, her head pressed against his shoulder. 'So you weren't with her on those nights?'

Blake gave a hollow laugh. 'I was in the office working,' he said. 'Or rather, trying to work. It was getting more and more impossible to sleep on that damned sofa with you on the other side of the door. It was driving me crackers, but I didn't dare rush you. I was afraid I'd killed any affection you might have had for me. You were cool and friendly, but I wanted so much more. So very much more,' he groaned, his hands moving under the folds of her flimsy gown to find the soft, warm flesh beneath. He bent his head and his mouth found hers in a long, clinging kiss.

'See what you've done to me by making me wake up and talk?' he muttered.

She pressed closer to him, her need rising to meet his, and his mouth trailed over her shoulders and found the hollow between her breasts. 'Oh, Maggie, my little darling, I love you so,' he murmured. 'I don't deserve you, but thank God your loyalty to the company made you turn up at the church that day.'

Her mouth twitched softly against his hair. 'It wasn't as simple as that,' she whispered.

He lifted his head to stare into her face in the moonlight. 'Why, then?'

'Because I loved you,' she admitted. 'I've always loved you.' She drew him closer as she whispered on a choky little laugh, 'How could I let you go?'

Harlequin Plus

A WORD ABOUT THE AUTHOR

Why is Marjorie Lewty such a romantic?

"It's all in the way you look at the world," she states. "Maybe if I hadn't been lucky enough to find love myself—in my parents, my husband, my children—I might have viewed the world with cynicism and written downbeat stories."

As it is, she loves to write about "what is surely the most important and exciting part of growing up, and that is falling in love." The happy ending is the beginning of something else, and like all beginnings, "it must hold hope and trust and promise and love if it is to fulfill itself."

Marjorie's writing career began during the Second World War, when she signed up for a course in short-story writing. Soon she was selling stories and later serials to magazines. Then she tried her hand at writing a novel, and as the title of her eighth Harlequin tells us, *The Rest Is Magic*.

Harlequin Presents

ALL-TIME FAVORITE BESTSELLERS
...love stories that grow
more beautiful with time!

Now's your chance to discover the earlier great books in
Harlequin Presents, the world's most popular romance-
fiction series.

Choose from the following list.

FAV-CB-2

ALL-TIME FAVORITE BESTSELLERS

Complete and mail this coupon today!

Harlequin Reader Service

In the U.S.A.
1440 South Priest Drive
Tempe, AZ 85281

In Canada
649 Ontario Street
Stratford, Ontario N5A 6W2

Please send me the following Presents **ALL-TIME FAVORITE BESTSELLERS.** I am enclosing my check or money order for $1.75 for each copy ordered, plus 75¢ to cover postage and handling.

☐ #17	☐ #35	☐ #41	☐ #66	☐ #73
☐ #20	☐ #36	☐ #42	☐ #67	☐ #75
☐ #29	☐ #38	☐ #50	☐ #70	☐ #78
☐ #32	☐ #39	☐ #62	☐ #71	

Number of copies checked @ $1.75 each = $ _____
N.Y. and Ariz. residents add appropriate sales tax $ _____
Postage and handling $ __.75__

TOTAL $ _____

I enclose _____
(Please send check or money order. We cannot be responsible for cash sent through the mail.)
Prices subject to change without notice. ·

NAME _____
(Please Print)

ADDRESS _____ APT. NO. _____

CITY _____

STATE/PROV. _____

ZIP/POSTAL CODE _____
Offer expires August 31, 1983   30556000000